OFUNNEKA

OFUNNEKA

Philomena Bivese-Djebah

SEVHAGE
PUBLISHERS

ISBN: 978-978-55559-5-0

SEVHAGE
An Imprint of VERSHAGE Enterprises

SEVHAGE
Suite 8, No 2, Ugbokolo Street, High Level
Makurdi, Benue State, NIGERIA.

Black Gate Trove, No 3, MFM Street, Karu, Nasarawa State

Administration and Correspondence:
SEVHAGE
C/o GERI, Suite 8, No 2, Ugbokolo Street, High
Level P. O. Box 2192,
Makurdi, Benue State, NIGERIA.

http://sevhage.wordpress.com
http://sevhagereviews.wordpress.com
sevhage@gmail.com
Makurdi. Karu. Abuja. Ibadan.
P.O. Box 2192, Makurdi, Benue State
+234 (0) 807 358 0365; +234 (0) 809 248 7425; +234 703 187 4471; +234 703 028 5995
Cover Design: Adakole Stephen & Su'eddie Vershima Agema

Dedication

To my late father, Chief Lucky Ossai Gabriel Ishiekwene, who is so exceptional and endearing, and his amiable wife, my loving mother, Mrs Silver Omede Helen Ishiekwene.

Chapter 1

She woke with a blissful start to survey her surroundings, uncertain where she was. Recollection flooded in like tingling sensations from a masseur's fingers. She had come in early the previous night for her brother's wedding. Exhausted by her tortuous journey, she had fallen asleep the moment her head touched the pillow on her mother's soft, comfy bed.

A night in her beloved hometown of Umuobi was always a thrilling experience. A town of serene ambience, famous for its warriors, it was founded by seven brothers. She had the most wonderful childhood experience here, growing up as the only daughter of Obidike, a prosperous descendant of the eldest of the seven brothers who founded the town. As a child, uncles and aunts pampered her to no end and every child in the town wanted to be her friend.

Ofunneka lay in the semi dark room for a while, revelling in memories. It was Saturday morning and she wasn't hurrying anywhere and her brother's wedding was not till much later in the day. Finally, she let her feet slide down onto the zebra-patterned floor as she felt for her slippers by the side of the bed. She slipped her feet into them; yawned and stretched, her long slender arm touching Otua, her mother's black bag hanging by the right side of the windowsill.

She looked up to see the bag and smiled. It was her mother's church meeting bag with all sorts of records kept inside. It was always by the windowsill, she recalled. As a child, she remembered how one day she had removed the bag from its position and incurred the ire of her mother. She had always wondered at the choice of location but never got round to asking or finding out.

She parted the curtains and opened the windows to let in a stream of the midday sunlight. She could hear the chatter of neighbours and children playing outside. She made to step outside but paused by the door and walked back again to stand in front of the large mirror by the wall. She stood there for some time, admiring herself, as the rays of light coming through the open windows created an almost overpowering silhouette of her.

Ofunneka was a beautiful woman in her late thirties. The years seemed to enhance her beauty; Ofunneka stood at 5 feet 9 inches with a pointed nose, big adorable eyeballs and lips as crimson as freshly plucked cherries. Her almost transparent light skin made it easy for people to mistake her for a mulatto. She also had a figure that drew eye-popping stares from men and envy darts from women. Some people called her *nwan miri,* child of the river, to the chagrin of her parents who harboured a secret they dared not disclose even to their only daughter.

She took off her nighties and threw on a strapless white top and jean trousers with sequins at the knees. It glittered with her every move. She adorned her slender neck with simple jewellery that matched her outfit. A sequined bangle and wristwatch completed the ensemble. She had an eye for fashion that complemented her looks, and on this day she looked good! She turned the key in the lock and stepped out into her father's compound. It was a block of four flats and a bungalow set back from the street and hubbub of the old town. She breathed contentedly in the warm sunshine before crossing to the block of flats where an elderly woman was seated peeling yams for lunch.

"Good afternoon, Mama Ifesinachi," she said, genuflecting at the same time.

"Ah, Ada, my daughter, how are you?" the older woman replied, smiling. "I did not know you were around, when did you return?"

"It was late last night, mama. How is Ifesinachi and the rest of the family?"

"They're fine, my dear. Your little daughter Ifesinachi will be very happy to see you."

"Yes, where is she?"

"Oh, she went to her uncle's house down the road with her sister. They will soon be back."

"Ok, mama I will see her later."

"Alright, my dear."

Ofunneka turned and moved with slow graceful steps towards the gate, picking up a white plastic water container on her way. Across the road, she stopped to buy snacks from Nne Ifeoma. She met Ifeoma, a girl of fifteen, who was excited to see her.

"Welcome back, Aunty Ada. I didn't know you were home, I would have come to sweep the house for you."

Ofunneka smiled at the girl who prided herself as her favourite.

"How are you, Ifeoma? Look how big you've grown. How's your mother?"

"Mother went to the market to buy things for the store."

"Greet her for me when she returns."

Ofunneka took some snacks from the showcase and brought out money to pay.

"No, Aunty Ada. Keep the money, it's my welcome gift to you."

"No, Ifeoma, take the money. You have to do accounts for your mother, you know."

"Aunty, you know if it's my mother she'll do the same."

"I know, Ifeoma, but your mother is not here. I will return when she comes back, but for now please take the money."

"Ok, Aunty Ada, thank you."

Ofunneka stepped out to continue on her way towards the stream. She had only moved a few steps when Ifeoma ran after her.

"Aunt Ada, I would like to come and see you at home later."

"Ok, Ifeoma," she said as she smiled at the teenage girl and rubbed her head affectionately.

She waved and greeted people intermittently, on her way. Most people in the town liked her, especially parents. They wanted their children to be associated with her. What drew such people to her was her humble, good-natured disposition. However, there were a number of her mates who disliked her. Some out of envy because they felt she was better endowed physically and got whatever she desired. Others were unsure of their reasons or were too ashamed to acknowledge them. Whatever the feelings or reasons, Ofunneka was a formidable woman.

She was wise beyond her years, a trait which several people agreed was an inheritance from her father. He would often tell her "The strength of a woman is not measured by the impact of all her hardship in life but by the extent of her refusal to allow those hardships dictate to her and define who she really is. His favourite pidgin expression was, "*Goat dey sweat na hair cover am!*" She grew up with the adage etched in her mind and learnt how to mask her pain under a cheerful façade. As she walked towards the stream, she remembered those words of her father and marvelled at how true they were, especially on this day. All she wanted was to find a quiet corner by the stream where she would be left alone to her thoughts.

The stream was reputed for its magical and healing powers. Situated at the heart of the town, with seven roads leading to and from the seven quarters that made up the town, it was the fulcrum of activities, next to the market. The names of the clans formed a song that children sang when they went for moonlight games. The song had its origin from the folktales of Enyadike, the legendary storyteller who no human eye had ever beheld. *Umuobi o, Umuossai o, Umudike o! Eh, eh, eh, Otutuoma, Umuazuka, Umuebenum Umuishioma! Ndi ne je ogbe ayin bu ofu! Ego, umu, esuieke bukor kor osayin...*

> *The children of Obi, the children of Ossai, the children of Dike! Good morning! Children of Azuka, children of Ebenum, children of Ishioma! Those who come to our community, we are all one! Money, children and health are for us all.*

Legend had it that in times past, the powers of the stream could help a barren woman conceive, if she simply swam in its deep waters. True or not, most villagers would attest that it had a most soothing vibe that could relax tired nerves. It was the reason why Ofunneka went there, to feel its calming influence.

Her dressing was a magnet that drew attention to her and hushed conversations, while raising comments; some complimentary, others derisive. Some were irked that a married woman with six children could still dress that way. They wondered if she was intentionally calling attention to herself and to what ends. There were whispers that she might actually be promiscuous but those who knew her well admired her style and carriage. The little children worshipped her. A few ran up to greet her. She in turn touched them affectionately and gave them some money. One or two grown-ups jokingly asked to share her snacks, which she ate along the way.

The sight of little children in swimsuits at the stream delighted Ofunneka. A flicker of a smile crossed her face at the thought: in her younger days, no one knew what swimsuits were. The children mostly swam naked or in their underwear while adults improvised with old clothes to cover their nakedness. As she stood watching the children, she noticed a couple of women close by. She walked up to them and greeted. Everyone responded, except Obianiberi, her childhood friend who had severed relationships with her.

"Obianiberi, I am greeting you," Ofunneka said.

Silence followed as Obianiberi looked away, her two hands supporting her chin.

"I don't really know what I did to you but whatever it is, I would like to know so I can at least ask for your forgiveness," Ofunneka said.

Obianiberi was not moved, even as the other women began appealing to her to respond.

Ofunneka continued: "For God's sake, Obianiberi we're not kids anymore. When will this enmity between us end?"

Obianiberi looked at Ofunneka, hissed and moved away. "What do you have against me?" Ofunneka persisted. "Even a thief is told his offense before he is punished. Have I stolen from you?"

"Is it by force that one remains your friend? Tell me, miss perfect life. Just leave me alone!" Obianiberi retorted. She hissed again and walked away, leaving a flustered Ofunneka behind. The women with Obianiberi eyed each other, either surprised or embarrassed by her outburst.

At this point, Ofunneka decided she had had enough and walked away. Before long, she was one of the few people left on the stream's sandy shore. She sat there on the sands, under the afternoon sunlight. Tears began to roll down her cheeks. *If only she knew, if only Obianiberi knew my share of pain*, she thought.

A scene from her past flashed before her like a movie. It was the rainy season. The leaves were green and luscious. Ofunneka and her friends played under one of the trees within the compound. It was drizzling and cold but they were too engrossed in their cooking to pay attention. Her mother, Otua's voice could be heard in the distance:

"Ofunneka! Ofunneka!! What will I do to you? I want to use that pot you've taken away from here..."

Ofunneka, oblivious of Otua's anguish, was busy at the back of the house cooking with her friends. Even at six, she was already practising how to be a mother. All the children in the neighbourhood were gathered at her house waiting for the yam porridge on fire to be ready. They were cooking with an old stove that took forever to boil water not to mention cook yam. But they seemed delighted with their progress. Above the clatter of plates and chatter of enthusiastic children, Ofunneka faintly heard her mother's call. She ran inside to answer and pleaded for more time to make sure the food was ready. At a point she started sharing the food. The children did not mind that it was not properly cooked as they were hyper-excited. Her mother needed the pot for the evening meal but she waited for Ofunneka because she welcomed the idea of her mates being with her to drive away the feeling of being an only child without siblings. She was constantly paying for her broken pots and plates that the children used to practise cooking; it was a small price to pay for her child's happiness.

That was how Ofunneka learnt to cook as her mother never allowed her do any chores. There were always aunts and cousins around who made sure things were done when her mother was indisposed. So, she learnt by watching them and her mother and practising behind the house.

Ofunneka gradually developed the habit of wanting people around her all the time. A messenger of the town's goddess had informed her parents that she was a future priestess of the deity, 'Nmo-Ndiobi' and had to be handed over for training. At the age of eight, she was to be presented to the shrine to serve as its priestess.

"No way! God forbid that I should hand over my daughter to any deity. God forbid!" Obidike, her father, had retorted to the messenger on more than one occasion. He was a devout Catholic and was not going to let his child be a priestess to any deity they did not believe in.

Strangely, no other child of theirs lived beyond two years. Several people attributed this to be the goddess's punishment for their rejection.

An elderly uncle of Obidike who felt worried by the death of their children had asked them to reconsider the goddess's request. But they were only too willing to suffer rather than tie the destiny of their child to any deity. Their daughter was too young at the time to know what was happening. Her parents ensured their house was filled with aunts, uncles and cousins, but they were seldom Ofunneka's mates.

However, there were pockets of unpleasant incidents. One day, Ofunneka returned home crying and would not be pacified, refusing to talk to anyone including Otua, her mother. She had cried all the way from her friend, Chichi's house. She could not understand why Chichi's mother did not like her as most parents did.

Her father was her best friend, even at the age of ten. He treated her as a grown-up and never scolded her, as her mother did, like a little girl. There was a special bond between father and daughter. When Obidike came home, he was told of his daughter's withdrawal and refusal to eat all afternoon. He went straight to her room. He had a manner of talking to her that seemed to melt away her pains. It was this charm he employed as he sat down to talk to her.

"Ofunneka nwam! Ofu ko ne ju akpati," he called. It was his pet name for her and it always pleased her exceedingly when he called her so. It meant *the single item that filled the box*. It didn't seem to work this time as there was no response from the figure lying as if asleep on the cute, pink-laced bed. He sat beside her, picking up her right hand and caressing it.

"My baby, tell daddy who made you cry today," he cajoled.

She turned to face him. The dried tears could still be seen lining her fresh, innocent face. Her father pulled out his handkerchief from his trouser to wipe what was left of the tears.

"Daddy," she said in low soft tones. "Is it true that I have bad luck?"

"No, Cherry pie," he replied, surprised at the question.

"Who told you that you have bad luck?"

"I went to Chichi's house to play with her and her mother chased me away."

"Why would she do a thing like that?"

"She said that I have bad luck. That I do not want to have brothers and sisters to share my daddy's money with me."

Her father's eyes flared in anger at such words from a mother to an innocent child, but he quickly controlled himself. He smiled at her.

"Daddy," Ofunneka queried. "Why don't I have brothers and sisters like my friends?"

Obidike was at a loss for words, but he continued to smile at her.

"Don't worry, your mummy and I will give you brothers and sisters."

She smiled and hugged him.

"Thank you daddy, I love you."

"Anything for my princess. Alright, come, let's go and eat."

It was not long after this incident, she recalled, that her baby brother, Enebeli, arrived. She was ecstatic and could not wait to tell anyone who cared to listen about *their* bundle of joy. Ofunneka grew up in such protected surroundings supported by her parents who spared no effort to ensure her well-being.

She also remembered her days at primary school. She was a member of the debating society and quiz club and won prizes for her school in competitions. She had teachers who came to the house to give her special coaching.

She was among the youngest who passed the entrance examination into secondary school. Her parents were overjoyed and Obidike decided she was going to a boarding school. Ofunneka was thrilled at the prospect of life outside the very protective setting she's been used to, but her parents were not. For the first time in their lives, they were visibly worried about her.

"What shall we do?" Otua wondered, afraid for her daughter.

"About what?" asked her father.

"She's only a baby; I can't bear to let her out of our sight."

"Oh, she's strong-willed, she'll cope alright. When she meets other girls her age, she will adjust," Obidike replied with a smile.

"Daddy," Ofunneka said, as she came in from the inner room where she had overheard some of her parents' conversation.

"What is the distance of my school from our house?"

She was dragging a box almost bigger than herself, some clothes and other items packed in it.

"Ada," Otua called, it was a name she used for Ofunneka when she was cross with her. "I told you to leave those things for me to pack."

"Mummy I want to pack them myself."

"Bring them here!"

She left the things on the floor and went back to get more.

Her father followed her with his eyes. He sighed and shook his head, tormented by the thought of his little girl alone in boarding school.

"What if she falls sick?" he wondered. He kept all his worries to himself, there was no way he would not share such thoughts with his wife.

Chapter 2

The school was a large compound with two gates at the entrance and three imposing buildings. It was an entirely new life but Ofunneka was determined to make the best of it. She was excited being among the few from her primary school that made it to the prestigious Epic Secondary School. What was most difficult for her was the morning call where they would be woken up by five o'clock to do various chores before heading to classes. There was also a compulsory one hour siesta observed in the afternoon, as well as reading preps in the afternoon and night. Depending on the day of the week, they had sports, labour and such other activities. Twenty-four hours never seemed enough but as the weeks rolled by, she got used to the routine.

At first, Ofunneka had a large group of friends and was social. However, she started paying more attention to her academics when the results for their first continuous assessment tests were announced. She had done badly. As her grades improved, her crowd of friends thinned down. This grew progressively worse as she advanced in class. She began to notice that she didn't share the same interests with a lot of her peers, one of their major interests being boys.

Since she did not have any boyfriend experience to share, she was not included in the girls' chatter. In her fourth year in school, something happened to her, which she didn't understand. She grew feelings she could not describe for a certain boy. Whenever she saw him, she lost concentration. She wanted the boy to notice her. She wanted to know where he went, what he was doing and who he was with. Whenever the boy played with other girls, she found herself disliking those girls.

One morning, the sun had just come out from behind the clouds. It was after the general assembly. She was about to cross the porch leading to her classroom when a shadow fell across her path. It was Ken, the boy she had been praying silently should notice her and who had refused to do so for months! She almost choked in panic.

Kenneth was a class ahead of her and by all indications, more mature. He was one of the more handsome and intelligent boys in his set and was liked by most of the girls who all wanted to be his girl. He had rebuffed all advances. He had eyes only for Ofunneka but waited to be sure she shared his affections. The day before, he had found out what he wanted to know from her friend who was his classmate and then made his move.

"Why do you like school debates so much?"

He had seen her once in one of the debates as she marshalled her points intelligently and had been impressed.

"I like talking," was her shy reply.

She was unable to look him in the eye but their friendship started that day. He noticed that she looked even more beautiful at close quarters and told her so. Her only reply was, "thank you." She liked being with him and being the centre of his attention. Most of the girls who had wanted Ken but never caught his attention became jealous of her. And the rumours started.

"They are jealous of you," Tony declared in his characteristic fashion as if his word would put off the misery. Ofunneka heard the rumours making the rounds. Some of the stories said that she was sleeping with Ken. Others said it was one of the Science teachers and that was why she was so arrogant and snobbish.

"I never knew that my friendship with Ken would bring such enmity from fellow girls, even some I thought were my friends."

"Well, you're only sixteen years old and still immature in the ways of the world. Don't worry, the gossips will stop."

She was silent for a while, deep in thought about what he had said. She hoped that he was right. She looked up and smiled at him in appreciation for his wise counsel.

"Where's Ken?" she asked. "I thought he said he would meet us here in twenty minutes."

"He'll soon be here, don't worry."

He looked closely at her with a mischievous grin.

"What is it," she asked. "Why that grin on your ugly face."

"I can smell love in the air," he said, laughing at her.

"Love? No, I feel deeply for him, but love? I do not know."

Tony had always been a good friend and confidant since their primary school days. Though he was her senior, he was always there like a brother to guide her. He was Ken's classmate and friend too. She relied on his counsel especially in matters of the heart, which she did not understand. She knew that the way she felt for Tony was not the same way she felt for Ken. It was Tony who explained these feelings to her. He also told her that her relationship with Ken needed more at this time.

"You've both gone steady now for a while and Ken will soon graduate, you know. What are you waiting for?"

She felt he must be right. He too had a girlfriend who was her classmate. But she was ill at ease pursuing those thoughts. Each time, her father's words echoed in her mind: "Don't allow any boy to defile you," he had said to her on several occasions.

It was early August and the rains had ceased for a while. The schools were on holidays and Ofunneka went visiting with a friend. Efe was one of the few friends her parents approved of, so during holidays the two girls usually exchanged visits. Efe's house became a meeting point for Ofunneka and Ken. She approved of their relationship and was urging Ofunneka to go beyond platonic friendship. On this day, Ofunneka's refusal caused a rift between them. Her holiday rendezvous with Ken thus ended abruptly.

Ofunneka also became friends with a girl who repeated a year in her class. She felt Beatrice was wiser and more mature. During Ken's final year in school she usually went with Beatrice each time he wanted to see her in school. On one occasion, they went together to see Ken. They were seated playing cards when Ken got up and entered an adjoining office. He called her into the office and told her exactly how he felt about her. The door wasn't locked.

She liked him, she was interested in what he was saying but her parents had warned her about such things.

"When we are older," she said, "if you still feel the same way about me, be rest assured I will marry you."

The conversation did not last more than a few minutes. They moved back to the outer room and joined her friend. Eventually, they left for class. The rumour mill started again. This time, the story was that Ken had had sexual relations with Ofunneka at their meeting place on the school premises.

A disciplinary panel was constituted to look into the scandal. Members were mostly teaching staff of the school. Ken was invited to defend himself. He told the panel that nothing untoward had happened between them and asked that she be given a mandatory medical test if they doubted him. But the panel was not impressed. The principal said it was the third time such a story was getting to his ears and wondered if Ofunneka was the only girl in the school. He said he never took the other stories seriously but this time witnesses came to testify that they saw them together. He believed this story had an iota of truth.

When Ofunneka was asked why she had entered an adjoining office alone with Ken, she was in tears and could not say a word. She and Ken were therefore suspended for a month.

It was too much embarrassment for her to bear. She felt disgraced. The girls who were excited by her suspension sang for her as she left the school compound in her father's car. Her father was embarrassed no doubt especially when he heard the part about entering an adjoining office, which she did not tell him.

"Daddy, I'm sorry," she apologized.

He asked why she couldn't explain to the panel.

"I was afraid they wouldn't believe me."

"I've told you, no matter what it is, never allow fear stop you from saying the truth."

"I'm sorry, daddy, for the shame I've caused you and mummy," she said, crying.

He stretched out his hand to touch and comfort her.

"I know you," her father said to her. "I love you, I do not care whatever anyone may think about you, and I know you more than anyone does."

Obidike had the option of going to tell the school authorities that his daughter was still a virgin but he considered the information a personal one. He therefore decided against it and told her to serve the suspension. But it became a recurring discussion in the family, whether they should have told the whole community that their daughter had not been defiled. Ofunneka's mother felt it was the only thing that could free their daughter from shame and public disgrace, but her father decided against it.

Ofunneka could not bear the shame, let alone repeating a class. It was not her fault. She was being unjustly punished. She was so distraught that she repeatedly thought of suicide. Her mother was at the verge of losing her sanity at the thought of losing her only child because of a useless rumour.

No one was aware of her attempts at suicide except her parents. At the last attempt, it took days for them to find her. They looked everywhere for their daughter to no avail. Then, a girl named Florence found her along a bush path far away from home.

Florence was from a family which was rumoured to have a shrine that needed young blood to thrive. Her grandfather was feared by the entire members of the community. His name was

Nohekogwan; it was a Benin name which meant one who takes his time to talk. No one in the community could remember when last they heard his voice. The man was weird and people were afraid of entering his compound. But his granddaughter was a good soul. She did not go to school on this particular day. Stories were told of how, long ago, enemies who came to the land were lured into the evil forest where they roamed endlessly without food and water and without finding their way. They were eventually strangled by the gods who governed the forest for disturbing their peace. It was not called *ejo-ofia*, evil forest, for nothing. That was the forest where Ofunneka was found. She would not have returned, for the gods of the evil forest neither knew son-of-the-soil nor foreigner. Florence appeared from nowhere to rescue her from certain death which she would have brought upon herself.

"The gods told me this was where to find you."

Ofunneka could only stare in amazement that anyone could find her there.

"If you had done what you planned to do, you would have burnt in hell, the gods had said."

Florence took Ofunneka to her house where it had been rumoured there was a huge shrine. To Ofunneka's amazement, there was none. What Ofunneka found instead was that Nohekogwan was a loner whom life had dealt a hard blow and wanted to be left alone. Florence, the only person living with him, had a place at the back of the house where she stayed without disturbing him.

According to Florence, the old man was like that because he went through a lot to put his children through school. Now, they were all overseas and none remembered or visited him. He became bitter and lonely and shut himself off from the rest of the people except Florence who was patient enough to understand him.

The two girls became the best of friends and Ofunneka's parents were thankful to Florence for finding their daughter and bringing her back to them. She became a regular visitor to their home.

The rains had finally ceased and it was becoming hotter under the clear blue sky. The change in the weather had also appeared to have transformed Ofunneka. She was in high-spirits and full of life. It was the beginning of a new academic year, months after the suspension. Ofunneka was back in school and so was Ken. She had promised herself to put everything behind and get on with her life but the girls at school were not making it easy.

Everywhere she went, people spoke in whispers; she could feel their eyes even when she turned her back. Her friends deserted her. She became a loner except for Tony and Ken but she was very careful not to be seen with any boy. Her parents had warned her to stay clear of all the boys, especially Ken.

Ofunneka told herself that the resentment she felt was of holy anger. She needed to prove that her downfall was not the end of the world. She was determined to prove she was better than the girls who ganged up against her. Her chance came eventually when the school authorities came to ask her to represent the school in the extra-curriculum activities she used to excel in. They didn't have a better replacement. She refused to consent to their request. Even her father was irked that they came to her when they could not grant her a fair hearing when it mattered most. But the school authorities kept on asking till her father yielded and asked her to agree. When she went for the competitions, her school, as usual, won with accolades.

The principal who presided over her suspension was posted to another school. The new principal liked her instantly. Some of the teachers had told him about her to no avail. He called her one day and said, "I like you. If you remain persistent, diligent and hardworking, you will be a star one day. Do not allow anyone to distract you. And remember to be prayerful." Ofunneka was thrilled by the words of her principal. It was all she needed from that point on.

She finished from Epic Secondary School in flying colours and gained admission into University of Bak to study Mass Communication. Ken had finished one year earlier and was working in his father's company while awaiting the processing of his visa to travel to the United States of America for his university education.

Ofunneka surprised even herself one Saturday morning when she visited Ken. He was alone at home, being the only child of his mother. His father was a polygamist and did not live with them. His mother had gone to the market to buy foodstuff.

As usual, Ken entertained her in the sitting room but suddenly Ofunneka got up, walked up to him and dragged him to the bedroom. At first, he did not understand her behaviour. It was so unlike her. It was when they got to the room and Ofunneka gently and methodically unzipped her jeans gown all the way down that he understood. Dumbfounded, he could only stare.

"Everyone assumes you had done it, now I want you to do it."

Her guts took Ken aback. He could still remember the first day he talked to her in school, how shy she had been and could not look him in the eye. He was uncomfortable with such guts. Though he had always wanted her, he never expected she could give herself to him in such a manner.

Ken was no virgin. He had had a few sexual relationships with some of the girls who threw themselves at him because he was handsome and his father's wealth was like an icing on the cake. But Ofunneka had remained his only girlfriend who had not allowed sex to be the determining factor in their relationship. He respected her for that. When the rumour mills started that he'd had carnal knowledge of her, he was only too sorry that they suffered for what they had not done. But that only helped to cement the bond between them.

Towards the end of his last term in school, when they came back from suspension, they were careful not to be seen alone to avoid another scandal but they had remained close. Now he was only too happy that Ofunneka has finally offered herself to him willingly.

He stared long and hard at the naked beauty in front of him, almost lost for words. He inhaled deeply. Ofunneka smiled as an invitation. He moved towards her with unsteady steps.

"O-f-u-n-n-e-k-a!" He said her name slowly as if he was savouring it.

On this beautiful Saturday morning in May, he could imagine firecrackers being ignited and their brilliant colours brightening the heavens and bringing a glow to the room, while a force as old as man began the slow unnerving off his senses. Ofunneka lying on the bed beckoned him to herself and appeared unearthly. It was as if he was in a trance, in another world where time stood still. He had dreamt of this moment countless times but never imagined that such a beautiful, ethereal creature would lie on his bed and beckon on him to come and take her.

Ofunneka watched with excitement the reactions she had aroused in him and was only too pleased. As he slipped into bed beside her, she caught the exhalations of his breath and thought to herself that the idea of being beside him in bed quickened her pulse too. His presence beside her, breathing in her ears, comforted her.

"Ofunneka," he spoke her name again as though reassuring himself that his voice had not left him. She was irresistible to his sight.

She responded by moving closer to him and whispering in his ears.

"Please take me, Ken, do it," she pleaded, afraid he might stop any minute leaving her wanting and confused.

Ken, his maleness rising with each touch, could not wait any longer. He thrust into her and suddenly froze, surprised. At the same time she cried out with much pain. He turned to look at her still surprised.

"Are you...? Haven't you?"

She nodded shyly.

"What!! I never knew, I'm sorry," he muttered, moving away from her.

"No, I want you to do it. I am eighteen for God's sake!"

She wanted him to come back, afraid he was rejecting her.

"All the while in school when you refused me I thought you were being tough. When I told them at the panel two years ago that you were pure, I never believed it myself but I just said that in your defence because I had never seen you with another man."

"But I thought ..." he silenced her with a finger to her lips.

"Say no more my darling, I love you. We will wait till we are ready for marriage. I vow this day to marry you. Wait for me, anywhere you are. Just wait for me."

Chapter 3

A few months after their vow, Ken had to travel to the United Kingdom to read International Diplomacy. He made a habit to keep in touch with Ofunneka, who got admission into the Federal Government owned University of Bak. Most of the girls on campus already had boyfriends but Ofunneka did not care and the other girls nicknamed her "receptionist." She was always the one who would be in the hostel to receive notes and messages from their visitors. Her friends thought she was pretending. They could not believe that such a beautiful, intelligent and friendly person like Ofunneka had not attracted the fancy of any of the numerous boys on campus. They felt she had a boyfriend she did not want anyone to be aware of. She confided in a few that she had a boyfriend abroad whom she had promised to wait for. Such confessions only elicited laughter and sarcastic remarks.

When the pressure became too much, she got herself a boyfriend even if only to stop the mockery of her friends. That decision marked the beginning of many mistakes that were to plague her life. Ashanti was one of the young men who tried to woo her. He was a picture of male beauty; with a well sculpted figure, well developed muscles, and an oval face that was near angelic. He had a rich chocolate skin which he took time to pamper. Ofunneka had laughed at his name when they met, noting that the name was more popular for girls. He had explained to her that though he was Igbo, his father had once been a diplomat in Ghana, which explains how he got his name. A lot of people had a different theory and claimed 'Ashanti' was a nickname he gave to himself to make himself socially relevant with claims to a Ghanaian heritage He was one of the most popular guys on campus but cool headed when it came to his studies.

His persistence and serious-mindedness toward his studies won Ofunneka over. So, when she decided to get herself a boyfriend, just so that her friends would stop mocking her, she settled for him. Soon, everyone knew them as an item on campus but she never once gave in to his sexual advances. She had promised to wait for Ken until he returned and intended to keep her pledge.

Ashanti was as persistent in his trying to get into her pants as he had been in trying to woo her, or even more so. He told her he was not cut out for platonic affairs. He also told her that it was his deep fondness for her that kept him coming back to her despite numerous turn-downs. Ofunneka suspected he had his way once in a while with some other girls but since she was not ready to give in to sex, she allowed things the way they were.

One Saturday evening, Ofunneka had a quarrel with her roommate. She stormed out of the room in anger and soon found herself walking aimlessly around the campus. Her walk took her towards the private male hostels. She was about to turn back but decided to visit Ashanti instead. She was not ready to confront her room-mate yet. Moreover, she had not seen Ashanti for days.

He was not in when she got there so she decided to wait. In the course of waiting it began to rain. It was in the middle of the rain that Ashanti finally arrived. It was a heavy down pour and he was thoroughly drenched. The rain continued late into the night, so Ofunneka could not return to her hostel. She decided to spend the night at Ashanti's room, something she had never done before.

They talked and danced and laughed and had some soft drinks. She soon forgot her problems with her roommate. Ofunneka had never tasted alcohol all her life and she could swear that alcohol was not part of the menu on this occasion. She could remember feeling a little dizzy but did not know exactly when she fell asleep. She woke to find herself naked and Ashanti smiling contentedly down at her.

She got up quickly and gathered her clothes about her before asking:

"What did you do to me?"

She looked at him with a plea in her eyes as if appealing to him not to pronounce the words that she feared. Then she noticed the wicked grin on his face.

"I put a little something in your drink to make you relax and you slept like a baby. My own baby. I took what should have been given to me a long time ago. Only I did not know it was going to be too much work. So you were still a virgin?" He said it without emotion as if it was an accusation. She felt deflated.

No, this can't be happening to me, she thought as she felt her world spinning. Ashanti had drugged her and taken advantage of her. *No, no, it was meant for Ken. I promised Ken I would wait.*

"Why are you crying?" he asked. "I helped you do a job and you're there crying."

The tears fell in torrents. She felt a stab to her chest and felt it twist deeper knowing that her supposed boyfriend did not care that he had raped her. She realised after some time that he was still talking:

"…and so please, I do not deal with inexperienced girls. I do not think this relationship can continue."

She got up and rushed to the bathroom. When she came back, he was standing by the window, his back to her. Without another word, she flung open the door and rushed into the chilling dawn. As she walked hurriedly along the narrow passageway that led to the female hostel, more emotions stirred inside her. She covered her face with her handkerchief so that those passing would not see her tears.

Weeks later, in her parents' home, she sat alone in the courtyard of the bungalow with its colonial architecture. It had become her favourite place of meditation. Her parents had gone out in the morning for a wedding. Today, her home's comforting beams could not provide the needed shelter from the turmoil she felt. She wished at this moment that she could turn back the hands of the clock.

Since returning from school, she wanted to tell her parents but could not find the courage to open up to them. She suddenly felt like throwing up and rushed to the water tap close by. She bent low and emptied her bowel, then washed the vomit away with water from the tap. She also washed her mouth and face. As she straightened up, she felt like fainting. Then, slowly, she walked back to the shelter and sat down, her head bent low. It was then that she heard her name. She did not react to it at first. The voice sounded excited but Ofunneka did not want to share in the excitement.

"Ofunneka?" that unmistakable voice queried. She looked up slowly to see Ken in a haze. She couldn't really focus well. Was it really him or was her mind beginning to play tricks on her like her body was?

He stood close to her, and her nose took in his signature perfume fragrance. Under normal circumstances it would have been very comforting but on this day it fuelled the nausea she felt, and she rushed back to the tap to vomit. When she collected herself she looked up to him with tears in her eyes.

"You've changed," was all he managed to say.

She sat down now by the tap holding her head in her hands and couldn't say a word. He looked at her long and hard. He did not like what he saw.

"You've given yourself to someone else." It was more of a statement than question. Ofunneka wept. She wondered why he had to return at that particular time. All the years he had been abroad she had dreamt of when he would be back. She had longed for his return and now he was back she was not happy to see him. The paradox of life! Fate had played a fast one on her. The excitement she would have felt had been replaced by a feeling of melancholy, a poignant feeling that was beyond description.

"Why?" he asked. "I kept myself for you, Ofunneka. Why?"

She cried the more. He sat down beside her and began to weep also. She began to explain the circumstances that led to her betrayal. Ashanti had drugged her and raped her. The man in question was someone she had been going out with. She had never wanted a sexual liaison. Now, how could she say to anyone that she was raped? It was after one month she realized she was pregnant and had come home to tell her parents but had not been able to do so. Since the incident between Ashanti and herself that night, he had not come to see her but had started going out with a smoking go-go girl on campus.

How could she begin to say *I'm sorry* to Ken? For the umpteenth time, she wished she could turn back the hands of the clock. Their dreams of having him be her first had been blown.

Ken could not deal with it. He could not comprehend that his angelic, Ofunneka had given what belonged to him to another man. He could not deal with her losing her virginity to someone else. And to make matters worse, she was pregnant by the bully that did not value her purity. He had been thankful to his creator when he realized she was a virgin and was hoping to come back and find her still intact. But now, he was at a loss even for words.

He suggested that she should terminate the pregnancy but she said she could not do it. She could not even bring herself to think about it or tell her parents. It would be a big blow to them. She thought of suicide. This would be the second season she would contemplate taking her own life. After only a brief reflection, Ken realized that he loved Ofunneka too much to see her suffer like this. He believed it was not her fault that things had turned out this way.

Then he surprised her.

"I will tell your father the pregnancy is mine."

Ofunneka was stunned beyond words. She looked up at Ken in disbelief and passed out. Ofunneka's parents could not comprehend that their well-behaved daughter had gotten pregnant before wedlock. They felt it was a betrayal of everything they had taken their time to teach her. "Where did we go wrong?" they asked themselves over and over.

Ken's parents were unsettled by the very thought of Ken abandoning his studies abroad to settle down for marriage at the age of twenty-four. His mother knew something was wrong but could not put a finger to it. Ken was her only child and she wanted the best for him. Marriage at this time was not what she had planned. He was supposed to go back to the United States and complete his studies. She even wanted him to remain in there after his studies and not meddle in the family business. The family was polygamous and he was the eldest of all the children. She wanted him far away from home because of the jealousy of the other wives who felt they deserved better honour because they bore many sons. She felt he did not know what he was doing by marrying at the age of twenty-four. Besides, she wondered how Ofunneka at twentyone could cope with pregnancy and her studies as she was yet to finish her university education. Ken however stood his ground. All his mother's entreaties fell on deaf ears.

His father was somewhat happy he was no longer going back to the United States. He could start work in the family business being the eldest of his sons and heir apparent. Their traditional marriage was done quietly, a sign of both families' disquiet.

Months into the marriage, Ofunneka became depressed. She couldn't sleep with her husband. This was not what she had dreamt of. It was not what she had envisaged their marriage to be. Theirs was a marriage built on falsehood. They had deceived their parents in order to get married. They had lied to everyone about why they rushed into marriage. She could no longer deal with the fact that she allowed Ken marry her while she was carrying another man's child. It was unfair to him. She was simply selfish. She felt wicked. She didn't understand herself anymore.

He was very patient with her. He loved her so much and could go to the ends of the earth for her if need be. He didn't understand why she was allowing guilt to destroy their happiness. Ofunneka's guilt trips became worse with the coming of the babies. She had twins, a baby boy and girl. Each time anyone commented on how they resembled their father she felt worse than ever.

Her guilt was eating her up. She lost weight with each passing day. She couldn't live with it anymore so she decided to tell her parents the truth. She asked Ken to let his parents know the truth, that their marriage was a lie.

Ken could not bring himself to tell his parents and it became a strain in their relationship. The issue became too much for them to handle. One day, she took the bull by the horns and told her parents. Obidike's reaction was not what she envisaged. He disowned her. He could not comprehend that his only girl child, the one he had brought up in good Christian conduct, would be such a disappointment and disgrace. How would he face his inlaws? He considered her wicked and in need of salvation.

Obidike had thought all these years that he knew his daughter, that the bond between them would have made her confide in him when it came to such crucial matters. He could vouch for her on any matter, but this? No, he couldn't take it. He thought no matter the kind of cover Ken had agreed to give her, she should have confided in him. He would have been very disappointed alright. But when he calmed down he might have sent her abroad where she could have had her babies and completed her studies rather than agree to Ken's marriage proposal and in turn ruin the boy's life. He saw her now as selfish and cruel. He didn't want a cruel child or anything to do with her again.

She was happy about one thing though; she had gone back to school after the birth of the twins. Her education had been very important to her. Her bequest could take her through school. She was already twenty-two and could spend her money whichever way she desired. She was also grateful to Ken. He had given what no man could have given to her – a name and had covered her shame. But she wanted them to start on a clean slate, on the foundation of truth.

Otua was torn between following her daughter and remaining with her husband. In the months that followed, she consoled herself with occasional visits. She would sneak away from home to visit Ofunneka and her grandchildren.

Ken's parents, especially his mother, was furious. They banished Ofunneka and her children from Ken's house and warned him not to have anything to do with her ever again. He was devastated. He loved her so much and believed that whatever had happened in his absence was not entirely her fault. He still wanted her as his wife but the pressure from the parents to desist from such foolery was too much. Besides, Ofunneka was not ready again to enter into a relationship not supported by both parents and so they parted ways.

Life became a succession of thorns for Ofunneka. She only lived through it because of her children. The twins brought succour to her; they became her safe haven, her comfort zone. She rented an apartment in a corner of the University town so that it will be easy for her to shuttle between school and home. Though she had a nanny who looked after the children, she tried as much as possible to be there at their every waking moment. Her mother was the only visitor she allowed in the house, the few occasions she was able to deceive her husband that she was paying a visit to her own parents. She would use the opportunity to see her daughter and grandchildren. Obidike had warned his wife on several occasions never to bring up the issue of her daughter and the possibility of rescinding his decision over her or else she would pack out of his house.

After two years, Ofunneka completed her course at the university and needed space away from home in order to reflect on her life. She decided to head to Ghana because of everything that the country stood for including its beauty and African heritage. Besides, it was an English-speaking country and she reasoned it would be easier to blend in. It would give her the anchor she needed to bring a semblance of normalcy back to her life. Her mother persuaded, cajoled and even cried, all in an effort to restrain her from going so far away. She wanted to be able to see her daughter and her grandchildren but Ofunneka had made up her mind. In order to pacify her mother she agreed to leave the twins with her in Nigeria. Though they were too young to be without their mother, the older woman agreed.

Chapter 4

The Boeing 747 touched down at Kotoka International Airport, Accra, as dawn smiled to a wet morning. With the coming of daylight the early morning drizzle had transformed into an irregular downpour. Ofunneka disembarked from the aircraft and surveyed her surroundings. She was neither afraid nor saddened by her new existence. She was glad to be by herself, living for herself, in a new world of fresh beginnings. She had withdrawn sufficient funds from her endowment. If she lived sensibly, something she could not lay claim to having achieved, she would probably be able to support herself fairly comfortably for another year, a year in which she would try to bring harmony to her life and forget the misfortune of the past. She walked slowly to the arrival hall after collecting her bags from the luggage area. She found a taxi without fuss, told the driver her destination and was driven off into town.

Ofunneka resolved not to be heartbroken. Every day, men and women went about their lives with broken hearts masked beneath facades of makeup and fine clothing. They put up brave faces, making the best of things, promising themselves time would heal their wounds. What else was one supposed to do? She had a conscience, even if that conscience drove her to exile, to a land where she knew no one and no one knew her. From there she filed for divorce and it was granted. This would afford Ken the freedom to start afresh and pick up the pieces of his life again. She prayed earnestly that he would find love and happiness. As the months passed, she heard from the grapevine that one woman had a child for him and was thankful to God. She decide to make her time in Ghana worth it. She took up a few courses in development and writing. She threw herself into it. In two years, she was done and picked up a job as a nanny in a school, to get in touch with loving and caring for children.

She started to keep a journal. Every morning before setting off by bus to the tiny school where her only companions were crying babies in need of their mummies and a change of diapers, she wrote it up. It was a chronicle, a way of charting both her work and her time in Ghana. Its random jottings and observations helped her to deal with the weight of her loneliness. She was away from her native country, a land of promise with an enigmatic people whose survival instincts were legendary. The Nigerian spirit lived in her for all of the three years she lived in exile. She felt she had in a way got over her past experience, but not the pain. The longing to feel the tranquillity of her native Umuobi, and her loved ones especially her children never ceased.

There were few nights when she slept soundly. Occasionally, she had nightmares and was woken, disturbed by her own weeping. Those dreams unsettled her, reminding her of her loss. On such nights, she longed for sunrise. She felt as though the cord that held her life had suddenly been broken and she was embarking on a journey, drifting downstream into unsafe, uncharted waters.

She threw herself into work. She needed to keep busy; it afforded her the luxury of forgetfulness. Apart from the crèche where she minded babies, she designed clothes. She had learned that skill from her mother and now used it to occupy her time. She also started writing. She published some of these and the diary she was keeping about her time in Ghana slowly transformed into a book. She wrote under a pen name. Her father had warned her not to bear his name again. The change of name offered her a more private existence.

Five years! Five years of her life had passed without her realizing it. It was as if time had stood still. The years she lived in Ghana were to her, years not lived at all. But time had moved on. The circumstances that took her to Ghana were still there but she was now more mature to tackle life. She was no longer the twenty-two year old girl who had married in a hurry in order to cover up a scandal. If nothing else, her sojourn in Ghana made her come to terms with herself and she decided to face the realities of life headlong and to move on. She heard that her mother was ailing and the doctors were worried about her chances of recovery. After much contemplation, she decided that her mother needed her. She prepared to return to Nigeria.

Ofunneka wondered about her mother's illness. It was at a time when her native Umuobi went through a series of calamities. When the young women of the village would get pregnant and lose their pregnancies in the seventh month. The priestess took time to find the cause and announced that the town was under a curse and needed cleansing. The problem, according to the priestess, was that a daughter of theirs was unjustly treated and until that problem was remedied the curse would continue.

* * *

An insect bit Ofunneka and she was shaken out of her reverie. She looked around, and noted that she was still by the stream with no one around. She wanted to stand up but had reached a point in her thoughts where things were becoming a bit clearer. She now knew why Obianiberi hated her so much. She was among the women who had lost pregnancies because of the curse. It was said that Obianiberi lost three pregnancies within that time. Obianiberi blamed her for her loss.

As realisation dawned on her, Ofunneka stood up and started running towards the direction Obianiberi and the other women who had gone. Then she stopped as a thought flashed through her mind: *What will I tell her?*

Part of the puzzle of her life was also the reason she never learnt how to swim. Each time she entered water she felt she was a fish and would quickly jump out. She often had dreams in which she had very long hair that touched her ankle. She remembered telling her parents about this and they dismissed it as mere fantasy.

There were numerous things she couldn't explain. For instance, when she wore jewellery especially gold, she would hear it fall and disappear. At times she felt as if someone shared her things, yet she never saw or knew who it was.

Another baffling experience was this: each time her children got sick and she gave them drugs they usually got worse. When she picked them by the feet upside down and spun them, they quickly got well. She didn't know why she did that but something surely made her do it. Whenever she listened to a particular traditional song, she would begin to hear voices and enter into conversation with those voices. Such experiences scared her so much that she visited a psychiatrist few times. It had not been of much help and she had stopped attending the sessions.

Leaving Nigeria the way she did, she was unable to find answers to those strange happenings. So, when her mother became sick, she returned. The joy of their reunion was unparalleled. When Otua saw her at the door of her hospital room, she jumped down from her bed and gave her a long embrace. Within days, she recovered from the illness that doctors feared was terminal. Obidike did not bother asking where she had disappeared to. They all just wanted to forget the past.

Otua was discharged from hospital in no time and they all went home. The mother had taken ill right from the day she left. It was only the twins that kept her going all those years. The twins who were two years old when Ofunneka left for Ghana could not recognize their mother. To them she was an aunt who had come to visit.

She took time to explain what had happened to her parents. She told the father it was because she did not want to soil his name that she had agreed to marry Ken under the circumstances. She did not know how to explain to him that she was raped and the person who raped her was her boyfriend. So, when good-natured, loving Ken showed up and offered to cover her shame she quickly agree but her conscience couldn't let her to continue living a lie.

They asked her to come and live with them. She refused at first but their insistence won her over. So, she moved in. It was as if she never left home. Her children became like her younger ones. People just assumed that it was her mother who gave birth to them because they had relocated from their hometown to Benin. Her father had bought a nice house in the government reserved area in Benin City. It was a fresh start for all of them. The children were bearing the name of her father. They called her "aunty" because everyone around them addressed her as such. So, she did not bother to correct them.

Everything fell into place. Not long afterwards, she started a relationship for the first time after all those years. She took time to explain to her new boyfriend about the children. She told him she does not know the whereabouts of Ashanti, their father. He said it was no problem but that the relationship between herself and her children should be kept as it was – siblings.

She wasn't particularly in love with the man, Amah Idige but was attracted to his sense of responsibility but as time went by she grew to love him. She began to notice how good-looking he was. Because of her past experience, appreciating men was difficult. She began to notice also that he had a good smile and was kind. She became attracted to him and they started dating in the real sense of the word.

One day, Ofunneka found out that Amah had been engaged to someone else but they were having some difficulties. This happened about six months into the relationship.

I can't do this, I can't compete for a man's love, she thought to herself. She tried to stay away but Amah refused to let her go. She believed in the adage, *The current of your stream cannot be too fast for you to drink from if it is yours.* She strongly believed in that adage. One day, she had decided to surprise Amah and showed up at his place early on a Saturday, only to meet the lady. The lady didn't wait for any explanation from Amah; she fought Ofunneka like a lioness. Amah was unable to do anything.

"What do you think you're doing?" was all he could say. When Ofunneka went home badly beaten, her mother nursed her wounds and forbade her from seeing Amah again. He came to plead but she wouldn't listen. He sent emissaries and he also sent his friends and relatives who knew her. She eventually forgave him but still, the other lady wouldn't let them enjoy the relationship.

Ofunneka could not understand what kept her in the relationship but because of the beating her rival had given her, she made up her mind that even if Amah did not eventually marry her she would make sure he did not marry her aggressor. And so, the table was set for a lot of intrigues.

Amah always made sure that before she came he cleaned and cleared all traces of his other woman. They kept on like that until Ofunneka insisted he had to make up his mind who he wanted. He settled for her and they were soon married in a quiet ceremony.

After marriage, she went to live with Amah in his family compound, a block of six flats where he lived with his brothers, their wives and children. She became the youngest of the community of wives but something was wrong. She tried getting pregnant but couldn't. She was obviously okay, having had children before. They underwent a lot of tests. They were both certified normal. Nonetheless the problem persisted. They both decided that at the appointed time, children would come.

One of the wives of Amah's elder brothers didn't particularly like Ofunneka. She saw Ofunneka as the evil one who had come into the family with ill luck. After all, the other wives had children. Each time there was a party, her children would not eat Ofunneka's food. Then one day, Ofunneka overheard her tell the children, "No matter how thirsty you are, don't drink her water, don't enter the house except I'm with you." She sighed.

Living with Amah in his family compound was a totally new and toxic experience for Ofunneka, but she decided that she had come to stay.

As time went by, she began to miss her children badly. Her husband had said they couldn't visit until they started having their own children. She usually went to spend time with them in her parents' house but she never stayed the night. There was never enough time spent with them on each visit since she had to hurry home to her husband. And it was such a long journey from Lagun where she lived with her husband to Benin where her parents lived. She was going through turmoil but she tried not to let it show. Once, she had told her father that she wanted the type of marriage he had with her mother. He smiled, then told her:

"My dear," he said, "What I have with your mother is special. You know me as your father and not as your mother's husband. As your mother's husband, I'm different. As a businessman, I'm different. If the men that do business with me describe me, you might not believe it's your father they are talking about. I am a man of many parts, as a father, as a husband and as a businessman. Maybe if you stop comparing me with your husband and looking
for my traits in him, it will be well with you."

She looked at him, puzzled as he sighed, then continued:

"Ofu ko ne ju akpati, nwam, there is no perfect marriage. You might not believe it but there have been countless occasions when we – your mother and I – were not the best we could be. But trust me when I say we have had countless occasions when we considered separation and even divorce." Ofunneka was shocked. She never realized that they had problems that could result in that.

"You see this your mother…" but before he could say any more, Otua interrupts.

"Please stop there, Chuks!" Ofunneka smelt trouble. That was a name she called him only when she was upset with him. "You know I'm the one tolerating you in this house. Your father has other women who he has even tried to get children with. For reasons I don't know, their children have kept on dying like my poor babies! Who knows, if not for that spirit or disease, maybe you would have had at least twenty brothers and sisters by now."

"Do not mind her," her father interjected. "Those were just away matches, there was nothing more to them."

Her mother recounted how he would go away from the house and pretend he had travelled out of town for business even though she knew he was in town with another woman.

"I never let you know of all these because I did not want to spoil the impression you had of him. We're telling you this now not because we want you to see us differently but because we want you to learn from it. Most marriages go through a lot to survive. We concealed a lot from you and that is why you have an illusion of a perfect relationship."

"Do you know how many times your aunt, your father's sister, Ndidi came to this house to clap her hands and ask me to pack out because she said I had become a mortuary?"

"But you're the one training auntie's children?" Ofunneka asked, her eyes wide open in surprise.

"Yes, I am. I'm telling you that Amah's brother's wife is just a drop of water in the ocean. Do you know how many times Ndidi came to this house to stay? Her lazy husband would not give her money. It's your father that pays their children's school fees, their house rent. Yet she'll still say I'm the one finishing their money.

As rich as your father is, even one house he has not built for me, at least not in my name." She turned to the husband, "Is it a lie? Yes, he will often ask me, *What do you need it for? After all, my own is your own.* It's only Ada I have for you. Tomorrow, God forbid, if something happens to you your family members will come and chase me away. I won't have anything. Yet, here you are telling me *My own is yours.*"

"Ah! Daddy," Ofunneka exclaimed. "You mean there's nothing in mummy's name?"

"When you people go to school you think you know everything," he said in response. But she was undeterred in her support for her mother as she knew her father was wrong in this situation. No woman deserved to be treated badly by her husband and her father was meant to do better.

"But you could write a will, let it be on paper, write a will daddy."

Obidike's eyes opened wide.

"Oh, you people want to kill me now, oh, I see."

"Nobody is killing you," Ofunneka retorted. "It's just that you should at least try and do the proper thing, you know I'm only a girl…"

"No, you're a special one," he cuts in. "You're one child that fills a box. Even if I had ten I would not have been prouder. It is not the number of children that matters. It is for the children to turn out right. When I tell people that I'm satisfied with only you they do not understand. I am satisfied with you. Yes we wanted more children but it didn't happen. It's okay. My wife and I are fine the way we are. You've given us extra children. What more do we want?"

Ofunneka listened keenly. She was happy that her parents appreciated her this much. If only her husband could do likewise. Maybe he did but was not a man of words like her father who knew how to shower her with accolades. Maybe she had been spoilt by her father and expected too much from her husband.

"It's only natural that we would want you to cement your relationship with your husband," Obidike said. "When your children start coming these same people will turn around to say you're buying children. So, don't let them bother you. When you can conceal your pain people look up to you and they envy you. It gives you a string to put yourself in check because you're already a model. Being a model is easy, sustaining it is hard. So, my dear, conceal what you feel. Don't tell people what you really think about them. They will use it as a weapon against you. Rather, just listen; without words nobody will misinterpret you. If you go and confront Annabel now, she would say that you're jealous of her because she has children. If you let her know that these things are getting to you she'll be happy. Pretend that you don't know she doesn't like you. She'll sit down in her quiet time and question her own sanity. Let her be the one worrying. Your conscience is clear and that's what is important."

What made Ofunneka run to her father this time was that a snake had entered the compound. Annabel used the occasion to emphasise to the other wives that since Ofunneka came, strange things had been happening. She said that Ofunneka was responsible for the snake in the compound and should be driven out. Amah was oblivious of this and other such incidents since Annabel always played nice to Ofunneka in his presence.

Ofunneka took solace in Prisca who usually brought her children for Ofunneka to babysit whenever she was busy. Ofunneka took solace in this noting that if she could be trusted with children then she was definitely not as bad as Annabel said. Prisca's children would spend weekends and half of their holidays with her. Annabel confronted Prisca during one of her visits.

"You have guts. You're not even afraid," said Annabel to Prisca. "What if she turns your children to something else? Or is it that you don't know where she's from?"

But Prisca refused to listen to Annabel

"Listen, Annabel, I haven't seen any reason to warrant my suspicion. Besides, God would not allow any harm come to my children. You might not have noticed but Ofunneka has a pure soul and because of that, I know, God will see her through."

Annabel was silent after this and never mentioned Ofunneka to Prisca's hearing again.

Chapter 5

The years piled on and Ofunneka found herself seeking more solace in God. She seemed a shadow of the purposeful lady who had returned from Ghana. She was not the church-going type but she knew that the spiritual controls the physical. God is spirit and all things come from Him. As a member of the Catholic Church she joined St Anthony of Padua Society and the Sacred Heart of Jesus and Immaculate Heart of Mary prayer group. Prayer to Our Lady of Perpetual Help gave her profound succour.

There was a time she was meditating when she heard a small still voice say: *You don't pray enough, you depend so much on yourself to do things. You keep looking for alternatives, I am the only source. There is no other alternative. Your parents have done their part. Their steadfastness and sacrifice have helped keep you. Now, you must allow me in faith to fight your battles, but don't tell me how to fight them.*

She looked around but didn't see anybody. She went to her parish priest to tell him about these things. She also complained about how her husband had been treating her. They were looking for the fruit of the womb but they hardly slept together. He was always running off for one business or the other. Even when he came home, the few occasions they were together, it was usually sex, not love making. She told the priest that she was thinking of quitting the marriage.

"The problem with most of you is that you do not understand the vow you took," the priest began. "You do not know the meaning of 'for better and for worse, for richer and poorer, in sickness and health, to have and to hold, till death do us part.' Let me share a story with you.

Once upon a time there was a couple that had been married for sixteen years. They had four children. Just like you, they fell in love, got married and started a family. She became engrossed in her role as a mother and wife. He worked tirelessly on his role as a provider. He was participating in his children's life but not as much as the wife. She became a stay-at-home mom, totally dedicated to the children. This couple did not take a whole lot of time to be alone with each other. Everything about them was with or for the children. Sometimes, the woman required more assistance from her husband but never asked because in her mind a good mother should be able to cope all by herself. Besides, she thought, he was supposed to offer his help without her asking. As the years rolled by, resentment began to build inside her, a feeling her husband was not aware of. Sometimes she would subtly relay her resentment, but not in ways her husband could relate to. After a while, she began to experience burn out. She started going out and disregarding how her actions affected her family. It was an emotional turmoil for her and her attitudes were out of character. She began with small doses of attention on herself and putting herself first. This led to an emotional affair. Luckily, it was discovered before she became sexually compromised. She was simmering with resentment towards her husband for his absence and lack of help around the home all these years. Her husband was outraged. He was a good provider and could not see why she was so upset with him. There was absence of trust and a sense of insecurity in the relationship. With the aid of counselling they both realized why the emotional affair happened in the first place. She

*had to appraise herself and realized that the affair was an escape
from dealing with her marital issues and her way of avoiding
conflict.*"

He looked her straight into the eyes and said:

"My dear sister, it is hard but I will ask you, to persevere and
stay in your marriage. Be like Joseph who trusted God and stayed
in his marriage to Mary when others might have divorced her.
Follow the example of Mother Mary, who remained faithful and is
today acknowledged as the Mother of the world. Be like Jesus
Christ who did not sin but suffered for the sins of the world. Pray
for your husband and for yourself. As Jesus tells us in Matthew
7:7, ask anything you wish of God in faith and believe He will
make it come to pass. Not in your own time, but in His own
perfect time."

She had replied with a quiet *Amen* and gone back home,
reflecting on his words. She took more time to pray and created
space for prayers in her life. This became a firm habit of hers as
she pushed on through the days that turned into months and years.

On a certain Sunday morning, about a fortnight to Christmas,
Ofunneka sat down in church with Amah. He had taken to
working from home for some time and it had given them more
quality time together. It healed the rift which was growing
between them.

Ofunneka quickly picked up the threads of her life and wove it
into something beautiful. She went into the fashion business and
had a fashion outfit. She designed clothes under the label,
Ladanelle Clothing. She was naturally a very creative person and
thrived in the fashion business. After a while though, she began to
suffer severe mood swings over the previous few months. One
minute she was weeping, complaining he was never at home, the
next she was despondent and nervy and over-sensitive. *Hysterical*
was the word Amah used to describe her state of mind. He was
very uncomfortable amidst all these and wanted her to stop. So, he
decided to stay home for the remaining part of the year. That

explained his being in church with her, which had not happened in a long time.

It was announced that Sunday that the church would organize a pilgrimage to Jerusalem for those who could go at the beginning of the coming year. Ofunneka expressed a desire to go. Her husband, to her surprise, decided to pick the bill. The promptness of his approval surprised her. She suspected he wanted her away so he could have time enough for some mischief. But since it was something she had desired for a long time, she decided to go anyway.

When the day came, she travelled with a group from her parish and other catholic faithful from around the country. When they got to Jerusalem she fell ill and couldn't participate in any of the excursions and programs. She assumed it was the change in climate that had affected her, staying in her hotel room most of the time to pray. The priest who accompanied them on the trip assured her that there was a reason for everything; all she should do was to be prayerful.

So, the others went out and came back each day to tell tales of the wonders of Jerusalem and its beautiful sites. She wondered why she left Nigeria in the first place. All she had managed to see was the airport and the hotel where they were staying. After two weeks they returned to Nigeria.

"So how was Jerusalem, did you see the holy places?" Amah asked when he came to pick her from the airport. She couldn't answer immediately because she was wondering how to tell him she did not see anything. He wondered why she did not seem excited. On closer scrutiny, he noticed she was not looking well. She then told him her experience, how she had been ill in the two weeks since they left Nigeria.

"After all the money I spent on this trip, this is what I get," he said jokingly.

"I've been really sick; I think it was the change in environment."

"Yes, you look harassed, I thought you would get some rest and here you came back sick. You've also lost some weight."

As he spoke, she began to feel nauseous and light-hearted...

She woke up to find herself in a hospital bed. She was told she had been out for about twenty-four hours. In that time, her husband began praying fervently for her recovery. He promised God that if his wife became well again he was going to be serious in spiritual matters.

Before she was discharged, the doctor came in to see them. He told her and Amah to sit. They feared he had bad news. But the doctor assured them there was no cause for alarm.

"Mr. Amah, your wife is not only pregnant but she's expecting triplets. That explains why she became so sick."

He wondered how she did not know. She explained that she'd been seeing her menstrual period regularly; that it never occurred to her that one could be pregnant and still see one's menstrual period. She had noticed it was not heavy but it still lasted for four days. The doctor said it was possible. Some women have such an experience. He told her that the journey might have added to her discomfort.

Amah was ecstatic; he could not believe that God would be this good to them. They were praying for a child, now he had given them three at once. He kept asking the doctor questions about what they needed to do. The doctor recommended complete rest for Ofunneka and told her to avoid anything that would stress her.

They moved almost immediately from the family compound to a duplex which he had earlier bought. Amah hired a cook, a gardener and a driver, all for her. She wondered why he had insisted they stay in the family house for so long. He said he believed that there was a time for everything in life. *If you don't go through one stage you wouldn't appreciate the next.* His father used to say, "You should bite a little at a time so that you can chew easily and swallow with ease," Amah said. His gesticulations as he spoke were really funny. They laughed like they hadn't done in a long while.

They started enjoying each other's company. Ofunneka's parents were ecstatic about the news of the pregnancy and the improvement in their relationship. Her children started visiting and life was good, very good. Amah kept his promises to God and became diligent in the things of God.

"I am God's biggest fan," he would say to anyone who cared to listen. Meanwhile, Ofunneka took time off her business to rest.

After nine months of blissful pregnancy, Ofunneka was delivered of triplets, two girls and a boy. The boy was named Daniel while the girls were named Daniella and Davina. They had a big party for their naming ceremony.

Amah initiated a number of development projects in Umuobi in honour of his wife. They built the town hall, built stalls in the market, helped ease the erosion problem that was disturbing the town. She had students from her town on her scholarship list. They called her mother a lot of adorable names for having such an illustrious child.

Chapter 6

O funneka's business, *Ladenelle Clothing* had suffered in her absence. She returned to it after weaning her children but things were not as they used to be. Two years could be a very long time, she realized, as she took the painful decision to wind down the clothing label. Later, she went into soap making. It collapsed too. She tried her hands on a few other enterprises that equally buckled under. She felt within herself that these other ventures collapsed because she wasn't really interested in any of them. She decided to become a stay-at-home mom.

Something of interest happened when she decided to become a home maker fulltime. Amah started coming home early almost daily. It was as if he secretly preferred having her stay home. She drew a food timetable, took proper care of the children and fell into a new routine.

But being an industrious woman, it did not take long before she got tired from being idle. She tried her hands on a few other things which did not work out either. In the process, she became pregnant again and had a baby boy, Ossai. She now had a total of six children, four for her husband, Amah, and the first set of twins she had before marrying him. Life seemed good.

Then it happened. Her husband came back from one of his business trips and started behaving strangely. When in her usual way she went to hug him, he brushed her aside in the presence of the children. She skilfully concealed her embarrassment and joined him at the table which was already set for lunch. He tasted the food and flew into a tantrum. She began to cry.

She couldn't just place where the problem was from or what had gone amiss. In bed that night, he just took one side of the bed and faced the wall, his back to her. When the children came to play with him he sent them away, saying he wanted to rest. She was really surprised by his behaviour but felt that the pressure of work was to blame. Then, slowly, things began to unravel.

They were in bed one night when a call came in and he tip-toed to the toilet to take it. He thought she was sleeping. This happened a few more times over the following weeks. Sometimes he would come back home at two o'clock in the morning yet he knew she wouldn't go to bed except he came home. She couldn't take it anymore. She told him,

"Rather than come home and you're not at home, I would suggest you stay wherever pleases you so that I will know you are where you want to be."

As usual, Ofunneka cried to her parents. They told her that the way she spoke to her husband was not right. They advised that even if it was painful, when he came home she should greet him and give him food to eat. Then Obidike, her father gave her another talk on marriage that kept her going for a very long time. He said:

"Marriage is for persevering women. The day you become impatient you're walking out of the door. You run to us each time you have a problem, if your mother was running to your grandmother, you probably wouldn't have known her. Now you can write your mother's biography, let your children write yours. So, my dear daughter, go back home. Biko."

"I am sorry Daddy but I am not going back home until Amah comes to plead for me to go back. Then I will know he is interested."

Obidike smiled at her like a child that knew little of the world.

"Ofu ko ne ju akpati, my dear daughter, marriage is about making up your mind and working towards your goal. I understand the pains I have made Otua to go through. I honestly do, and I do not really tolerate her faults. But you have to realise that success is an all-round thing. It is not just building a business, climbing the career ladder or making lots of money. Success is allencompassing; good background, good education, and stable home. Marriage makes it complete. Being able to bring up your children under one roof made it a complete story. Except you're at the verge of being killed by your husband, that is your life is threatened, I don't think any reason is good enough to leave your marriage. All these things you're saying, your mother experienced them too. Now you run to her, why? Because she is successful. What would you tell your children?"

"Ah ah! Daddy, no! Tell the children? Do you want me to go insane before you realize that I have a problem?" Ofunneka asked.

"You won't go insane," Obidike responded. "If you insist on calling it a problem, you're being negative. Just say your marriage is going through challenges. A problem means it's damaged for good. Say there's a temporary setback, there's a strange woman in your home. Find the right words to qualify her. Strangers come and go, the owner of a home stays."

Otua interjected here: "When it comes to strange women, there are some whose mission is to see that relationship between the couple is destroyed. The devil uses them to try and turn your day into night and you don't want to allow them. You can never go wrong on your knees, my daughter."

"You see your father, forget the fact that we are now talking like this, it took the grace of God to stay on. When I was shaking my waist on our twenty-fifth anniversary, when I was dancing and moving about joyfully, I was asking, where are those women today? That was my thought and I want you to think like that. Our thirtieth anniversary *nko*? Did he stop? If it was not one woman it will be one in-law or a neighbour or his business. The challenges will come. Have you forgotten your faith, your Catholic faith? It says, take up your cross and follow me. You say you're a member of St Anthony of Padua, Sacred Heart of Jesus and Immaculate Heart of Mary, and you have taken our Lady of Perpetual Help as your patron saint. Do I need to outline what they all stand for? St. Anthony of Padua, for instance; Look at the challenges he went through but today you're all following him because he persevered and became a saint. What about Jesus? If he did not defeat the cross to rise from the dead we wouldn't be Christians today. What does the cross symbolize? Dear, go down on your knees and I need you to understand something: It's not only when you have challenges that you pray. In season and out of season, pray to God. Cover your children, your husband and yourself with prayer. As your mum, let me suggest a prayer I use for our family..."

A prayer for help:

Dear God, give me strength to face each day and to see the many blessings that it contains. Give me the courage to walk on, no matter how long the path or how many turns the road holds. Guide my thoughts so that I walk in love and peace and with gratitude stamped on my heart.

Protect my husband and children as by blessing them you also bless me. Make their lives long, healthy and happy, and once they are grown, bless them with children of their own; strength to carry on in my absence; and knowledge that they are deeply loved.

Ofunneka who had been listening with rapt attention now interjected. "I wanted to tell you about the children also. Nowadays they listen more to their friends than I their mother. I feel I'm losing them. It is terrible enough that I am not on the list of good wives. If 'bad mother' is added to my credentials, I would feel as good as dead."

"The mistake you young parents make is that you forget you were once children." This was coming from her father. You should learn to think the way the children think. Go back home; change your method of talking to your children. Nowadays it is worse than when you were a child. They are privileged to have a lot of information. If it is not Internet, it is television or one of those high technology devices in existence now. In your days you came to us to ask questions but now the information is everywhere for them to pick from and they may be exposed to the wrong kind depending on who is giving it. It is not in your own interest that they learn certain things from somewhere else. So, my dear, you have to go back even if it is only in the interest of those children. Keep using the prayers I gave you and add your intentions at every mass. God is faithful.

She started to ask how she would carry her things back when her husband did not come to take her back. Her father said, "Yes, I'm sending you back. Swallow your pride, it is not important whether he comes or not. The dung of a cow is manure to a plant. You should go back."

"There's something you need to do when he's ranting. Imagine yourself with a stone in your mouth. Imagine yourself in a hall that's noisy, so, you don't hear him, you don't speak, you just stare." She wondered how she could do a thing like that. Her father replied, "Nobody quotes silence, I need you to be silent at such times."

"But he's wasting the food, I would cook and he wouldn't eat," was Ofunneka's reply.

"Still he comes to the house, doesn't he?"

"Yes."

"When he comes, greet him. Welcome him. If he doesn't eat put it in the fridge, eat it the next day. You're always having guests, give it to them, it is in your place to cook."

After the talk, Ofunneka took time to pray and meditate on all she had heard. After a long period of meditation, she decided she was going to make things work. With this resolution, she sighed and found sleep.

Chapter 7

O funneka went back to her husband's house with head bowed. Amah was driving out and caught up with her by the door of the house.

"Why are you here? I thought you were gone."

She didn't say a word. He had stopped eating her food and did not ask her for anything. He didn't seem to care for her and never asked after her health or wellbeing. All he did was leave money on the dining table for her. He did not ask after the children's welfare. He did not attend their school games and other social activities. Even when he was invited, he always came up with one reason or the other not to show up. On a few occasions, Ofunneka cajoled her brother to join her during some of the events at the children's school. She figured they needed a father figure. Besides, she didn't fancy the idea of showing up at such events like a single mum.

That evening, Ofunneka cooked and served Amah's meal, then called him to the dining table, where she sat waiting.

"How am I sure you prepared this food with your heart?" he asked, when he finally took his seat.

"So, it has become so bad that you couldn't even call to find out where I was?"

"When a woman packs her things and deserts her matrimonial home, then she sure has a destination."

"Do you know why I came back?" He suppressed a mischievous grin but remained silent.

"I returned because my parents who should accept me would rather have me here with you."

"If you knew that, you wouldn't have absconded in the first place," Amah replied.

"My idea of marriage," she said, "is not to hang in there just to bring up children. There should be communication in marital relationship. What we want is to enjoy each other and build a good foundation for our children. I never anticipated for once that the kind of marriage I desired would exist only in my imagination. Sometimes I talk aloud to myself imagining who I am having a conversation with."

"I don't understand what you are talking about. I come home, don't I?"

"You come home grudgingly. You are home but you are absentminded. When you are not at home, I know you are not. But to be home and remain inattentive and aloof to me and the children is a torment I would rather do without. Sometimes, you even grin in your sleep as if you are enjoying this turn of events…"

"You have such a fertile imagination," he interjects, "why don't you use it creatively? I do not know what you are talking about." He picked up his car keys.

"Are you going out?" she asked in a shaky voice.

"What does it look like I am doing? I am off."

She cried and cried and then called her parents. Her father said, "I have told you times without number that marriage is for persevering women. It takes a faith-filled woman to absorb its shocks. Heroines are not made from lack of challenges. It is their ability to brace up to and overcome challenges that marks them out." He told her that she should find a convenient time to come and see them.

"You can tell him that I sent for you. Let him be aware that you are coming to visit us".

When her husband came home, she told him that she had to see her parents urgently.

"But you just came back," he said.

"Yes, I don't know what has happened. Father called and asked me to come as soon as possible". For the first time in a long while, she could feel his concern. She quickly called her father to tell him when she would be arriving. The next day, Amah offered to drive her down. When they got to her parents' house, Ofunneka's mother feigned to be seriously ill.

Amah sympathized with his mother in-law, gave money for medical care and left.

"Remember when you were ten and you suddenly had a little brother? You believed that your father had given you a brother as he promised. You were ecstatic and could not leave the baby alone". "Are you referring to my brother Enebeli?" Ofunneka asked.

"Listen to me; you do not know the whole story. A lady came with him and said he belonged to your father. I knew he had a few affairs on the side but to bring a child from outside was a new dimension entirely. I wished at that time that he would sleep and not wake up. The woman made so much fuss. Whilst I was trying to conceal our shame, she was busy announcing to the whole world that my husband fathered her child. For some reason I could not fathom, I knew the child was not your father's. But what betrayal culminated in bringing an innocent child to him to father? In the end, I took that child in whether or not he was your father's. The child did not ask to be born. I decided to take care of the baby but not under our roof. That was how your brother Enebeli entered our lives."

Ofunneka was speechless. She recalled that as a child she had sensed that something didn't quite add up about Enebeli. But she was only too happy to have a sibling to care for. She travelled back through time as memories of their childhood came to her. Enebeli was one of the best gifts life had given her. He had changed their world and...

"Then I went on my knees," Otua said. "I was on my knees telling God that this cross was too much for me to bear and God in his infinite mercy came to my rescue. The woman who brought the child took ill and no one knew what was wrong with her. Sensing that she would pass on, she called us and asked for forgiveness. She confessed that the child was not your father's but she wanted her son from another man to come and inherit Obidike's empire. She also desired to drive me away from my husband's house. She said what she did not understand was what Obidike felt for me. In spite of all she did to break us up, we remained together." Ofunneka suddenly found her voice.

"You mean she confessed to all that? Does Enebeli know this story about his mother?"

"No, he doesn't. There was no need to let him know. Anyway, the woman asked that I should forgive her; she said I have a pure heart. She appealed to me specially to take care of the son because we are the only family he knew. So, when he was grown to secondary school age we sent him abroad for studies. We often travel to see him. I call him my son. You see him as your younger brother and that's all that matters."

Other things had happened during that visit and Ofunneka resolved to make her marriage work. When she arrived their house, she made strides to be a stronger woman and her husband seemed to change towards her. Things had changed for the better with them, and for her brother, Enebeli. The years had been kind and Enebeli was now getting married. She almost couldn't believe it.

Ring. Ring. Ring. Ring.

The phone rang two more times jolting her out of her reverie. She brought it out of her pocket and smiled when she saw the displayed name of the caller: ENEBELI.

"Where are you?" It was the voice of her brother, Enebeli. "We've been wondering where you've been for hours now. Are you okay?"

"I'm on my way."

She stood up to behold the purity and calmness of the stream once more. This was what she loved most about her native Umuobi; to be by the stream all alone, to feel its calmness, and to be enmeshed in its purity and clearness. She walked towards the water, scooped some water with her two palms and washed her face. She said a silent prayer: "Lord, you are the source of life. You made the beautiful trees and their luscious leaves. You've always been there for me but this is bigger than me. My younger brother is getting married in few hours. I don't even know the right time to let my family know what I'm passing through."

She paused, surveyed her surrounding, and scooped more water from the stream. She smiled as she thought of her husband.

"Things are so wonderful with my husband and I right now. We enjoy each other's company. The children are grown up but not enough to be on their own. Lord, give me the enablement to sail through and be able to take care of these children because they need me. But Lord, let your will be done."

She left the stream, walking leisurely through the footpath with the balsam or 'touch- me- not' flowers generously sprouting on both sides. She smiled as she recalled how she used to touch them on her way to the stream as a child, and how they responded by folding their leaves shyly. No wonder they were called touch-me-not.

"God you're awesome!" she said aloud, "There's nothing you cannot do."

She glanced at her wristwatch, surprised it was already past noon. She had been sitting there for hours and hadn't realised how far time had been gone. She walked out of the footpath onto the main road and hurried home.

Chapter 8

The sun seems to shine brighter in envy on some wedding occasions as if competing with the bride and guests. So, it was on this day as people gathered in different brilliant attires for a wedding. It was late afternoon and family and friends were already gathered in Obidike's compound in various colourful attires, ready to proceed to the bride father's house when. Ofunneka got home from the stream and greeted those she came across. She had left unnoticed earlier that morning and a lot of the visitors had been asking after her. The prospective mother in-law and the bride were there in their home, since their houses were a walking distance from each other. They strolled in to see if they could help do anything before the ceremony.

"Aunty Ofunneka *Otofe*, we didn't know you were home, my mother and I have been asking after you," said Iza, Enebeli's fiancée as she bent to greet Ofunneka.

"Iza, my wife, how beautiful you look, you ought to be getting ready now or is today not the D-day?"

"Yes, I will soon be going home with my mother to get prepared, we wanted to know if everything was in order here."

"You have done very well. Thank you."

"*Otofe* ma." Ofunneka was now greeting Iza's mother who was busy arranging cutlery set in a basin. "*Mama, I dey greet you o, Otofe.*" She turned to see Ofunneka.

"Ada, my dear," she saluted. "I've been asking your mother about you. How are you? How are the children? You didn't come with them?"

"No, mama they are in school now, they're not yet on holidays." Ofunneka entered the house to change. Everywhere was gay. Ofunneka's mother was all over the place making sure things were in order. She was visibly happy and excited. She was going to bring home a wife today; she was going to add to her family.

"My wife," she called Iza, beckoning her to come and help her lift a pot from the fire. Iza's mother was nearby and jokingly said, *Una never pay oh!* Another woman nearby replied, *In-law, even if we never pay your pikin na our wife now o.*

"No mind me, in-law, for this family I go give my daughter free."

They all laughed. There was camaraderie and happiness everywhere but Ofunneka was not part of it. This was so unlike her. Her brother observed her mood and knew something was bothering her. She was not her usual, vivacious self at this occasion. Ofunneka was the heart of every party. She was the one who usually made things lively, putting everyone in a happy mood. Enebeli opened the door to his sister's room and found her sitting on one of the couches staring into space.

"Big sis, what is the matter?"

She was nudged back to the present. "Nothing," she replied. "Have Iza and her mother gone back to their house? We should be getting ready now. Thank God you're already dressed."

But Enebeli was not fooled. He knew something was disturbing his sister. He sat on another couch facing her.

"Big sis, tell me what the problem is. In the last four years since Papa died you've been very strong, telling me all the time that papa is always here with us."

"No it's not Papa. I'm already used to the fact that he is not here anymore and mama is doing well. Look at her; she leans on God for support."

Enebeli interjected. "You made sure I lacked nothing. You simply took papa's place. I don't understand what is happening now but I know you're disturbed about something."

"Is it showing? Then I must be losing my head."

"No, you have a way of putting up appearances; Public smiles and private tears. Sometimes I see through it. Sometimes I don't. Are things going on well with you and uncle? Is it the children? What is it?"

"Nothing is going on. It's probably fatigue." She gave her brother a big smile.

"No," Enebeli said, not wanting to be put off by her smiles. "You were at the stream this morning, were you not? That's where you were when everyone was asking of you, and I called you. Anytime you have big issues you go there to clear your head. Remember when papa died? You went to the stream and stayed hours on end. I could still remember that day, I wanted to come and bring you home but mama said I should let you be. You've never stayed out this long by the river."

Enebeli looked worried and ill at ease.

"No, my brother. It is nothing. Do not bother yourself too much about me, I'm fine."

Once more, she changed the topic in order to take her brother's attention away from her.

"You know there are things we've not cleared, the caterer ought to be here by now."

"Yes, I've already sent them over to Iza's house."

"What other things are still outstanding?"

"Mama has taken care of things. It's left for you to get ready so we could proceed to my wife's house." She laughed.

"I like the way you said *my wife*, but remember you are yet to pay the dowry o."

He started laughing as well and shaking his head. "Big sis, you know now, we are equal to the task."

"Please husband, leave me alone so I can get dressed. Congratulations anyway, you have a good eye. She's a pretty girl."

"Thank you sis." He left the room. He felt happier seeing her laugh. He was worried sick when he found out that she went to the stream that morning. He prayed for whatever it was that was disturbing her to just go away.

Ofunneka got ready for the wedding and tucked away her problems.

The wedding turned out splendid. There were lots of people. Many of their relatives she hadn't seen for years were there. Even their friends from Omiako came to grace the occasion. She was especially happy seeing Otua, who she has been worried about, in such joyous mood. She had always felt that a part of her died with her father, but today she seemed exceptionally happy.

The day was long but the ceremony went well. They finished late in the night. The bride was escorted to their home. The entourage that came with the bride was entertained and given places to sleep.

In the middle of the day Ofunneka felt a tap on her leg. She woke with a start and sat up. She saw him sitting right there at the edge of her bed like he used to all those years. He said to her, "It is well my daughter. Everything that has a beginning has an end."

"Papa this is too much for me. We're talking about life and death. You used to tell me that when there's life there's hope. This time I'm about to lose mine. I don't know if I can make it, I don't even know what this treatment would do to my body."

"God does not give you what is beyond you to carry. You'll sail through."

"To even say the word scares me, papa."

"Say it, it doesn't change anything. I urge you to say it."

"Breast Cancer," She said quietly and in that second, it seemed as if a heavy load was lifted off her shoulder. She felt lighter and she began to cry. She could feel her father hold her. She felt warm in his comforting embrace and she felt like a child again. It was as if the embrace erased all wounds and pains. Then the door opened and her mother stood there looking at her with a surprised look on her face.

"Who were you talking to?" Otua asked coming into the room. "What is going on here that you are beginning to talk aloud to yourself? Ofunneka, I'm your mother. I should know."

"Nothing mama," she said, drying her tears so she would not see them.

"No, you should tell me what it is! Except you want me to join your father. I have lived my life, I have grandchildren, so if you want me to join him this night, feel free."

"Okay mama, I will tell you when it's time."

"That's the thing you have in common with your father. Nobody pushes you to do what you do not want to do but this time I need to know. All my life I've never heard you talk to yourself. A few times maybe. Like when your father died. But this one in the middle of the night?"

"Don't worry mama, I will tell you, go to sleep, tomorrow morning I will tell you, I promise."

Though rattled, Otua went back to bed to wait for dawn.

The next morning before Ofunneka could come out from her room, Otua and Enebeli walked into her room. She was startled as she had not locked her door the previous night. She looked at both of them wondering why they had decided to barge on her at such an early hour. Both were unable to conceal the worried expressions on their faces. Without any pleasantries, they told her they needed to know what was happening to her. She didn't mince words this time. She couldn't keep it from them anymore. They were her family and they needed to know. Even if she was dying they had to know.

"There are indications that I have some biological changes that are not normal, she began. "So I had a mammogram. When the result came out it was positive. I am going to undergo breast cancer treatment..."

She had not finished speaking when Otua passed out. Enebeli was completely devastated. When she eventually came round, Ofunneka sat beside her in the hospital.

"You see why I didn't want to tell you?"

Otua heaved a big sigh. "I lost my husband. Will I now lose my child while I'm still alive? What am I living for then?"

"You are not living for me alone," Ofunneka admonished her. Enebeli wanted to say something but changed his mind.

"Please, this is neither the time nor the place for lamentations. Mama I beg you, do not make my faith falter."

Enebeli eventually found his voice. "You know you are the hands and legs of this family, I am not you. Where will I begin from? I don't have your sense of organization. I don't have your endless love. You are always there for us even when you are uncomfortable. What do you want me to do? This is a mantle I cannot handle. Papa gave it to you because he knew you were capable. Please don't give it to me. Not now. Not for a long time to come." He stopped for a while with head bowed.

"Have you told your husband?" he finally asked when he raised his head. He had tears in his eyes. Ofunneka saw the tears but resolved not to let their emotions get to her or else she would become incapacitated even before commencing treatment. "No," she answered.

"You have to," said her brother.

"I know. It's a problem disclosing this to him considering how he would feel. We've grown so much over the years to come to love each other that I know without me there's no him. It wasn't like that at the beginning. There were moments when I wanted him dead, when he caused me so much pain. It took the grace of God to forgive him. But over the years he did make amends. The saying that it takes a woman for a marriage to work is true. But it does work well with the support of the husband. And that is what our marriage has come to stand for in recent years. Now, just when it's near perfect I am at the door. How am I supposed to feel? Our children are young. They've grown, yes, but they still need me. The twins now know that I'm their mother. There was no need of explanations because it didn't make much of a difference to them whether I am their mother or their sister. This is the time Ifeoma needs me to guide her. She's into a serious relationship. She will get married someday and maybe I won't be there."

"Big sister, why are you talking like this? You were the one who said this is no time for lamentations."

Ofunneka continued as if she had not heard him.

"Consider my son, Ossai; he is neither here nor there. He feels as if he's a big man yet he's not really a man yet. What about the other children? What will I do? I will go for the treatment and once I start this treatment my system may begin to pack up. What do you want me to do?" She was near tears now.

Otua was screaming again. The nurses came and said the children should leave her alone to rest but she refused to let them go. When the nurses had calmed her down, Ofunneka's speech turned to words of exhortation.

"I'm using my last energy to do this. Now everybody should live his or her life like he may not see tomorrow. In case I do not survive, I want you people to remember me as the one who had a free spirit; beautiful and appreciative of life. It may have been short but I had a formidable life."

Enebeli was unhappy that his sister was referring to herself in the past tense. He cautioned her mildly to desist. He called his wife to come to the hospital and told her that their proposed honeymoon would be suspended. "I will give you the details later," he told her. "My sister and I, including yourself and mother, will be heading to Lagos immediately."

He turned to his sister, "We would be flying to meet with your husband. You won't be taking your treatment in the country, not because they won't do a good job here but because I need to care for you. I'm a doctor for God's sake. I have colleagues who are specialists abroad. They can take care of you. My wife and I will go with you to give you emotional support. If we can afford it, let's not take any chances."

It was a rather long speech coming from Enebeli. Ofunneka could see that her baby had gone into command mode. She was glad.

"Before travelling out for the treatment there were a few things I need to take care of". Ofunneka said. "Some of my friends will be marking their fortieth birthdays over the next few weeks. I intend to be there."

"For what?" Enebeli asked, irritation clearly etched in his voice. He was irked that her sister was talking about birthdays and parties at this time.

"It's a reunion. We promised ourselves ten years ago that if we get to be forty we'd all have dinner together, take time to share our experiences and take stock of our lives. We've kept in touch through phone calls and e-mails but we've not seen each other as a group in a long time."

Funmi, one of them, had passed on in the interval. The party was partly in her memory. Plus, they planned to raise some funds to be given to Funmi's eldest daughter to help in her siblings' upkeep.

It was agreed that for mama's peace of mind she would travel abroad with them. Enebeli suggested that Ofunneka should tell the children she was going abroad for a master's degree programme. They would understand because she usually went for training abroad for periods of six months or so.

They chartered a vehicle and made Ofunneka as comfortable as possible. On getting to Benin where Otua and Enebeli lived, they packed what they needed for the journey and continued to Lagos. Ofunneka's husband, Amah, was not in town when they arrived. He had travelled on a business trip to the United States of America a few days earlier. She called to tell him that she would be joining him in a fortnight. She did not want to disclose the reason for her trip on the phone, but made him understand the urgency of the matter. She planned to visit the children in school before travelling out. The Reunion party was in five days' time.

That evening, just before dinner, all four of them - Ofunneka, Otua, Enebeli and Iza his wife - sat in the sitting room watching movies. The newly wedded couple tried to make everyone comfortable. They recounted how they met during their school days, places they visited and friends they had in common. No matter how interesting their stories were, there was a cloud of heaviness that wouldn't lift.

Throughout the period they spent waiting for the US embassy to finish processing their travel documents, the atmosphere was charged with a poignant sense of foreboding. Enebeli prayed frequently that "There shall be no loss." Mama's favourite expression became, "I shall not bury my child, God knows I shall not."

"It is not the end yet", Ofunneka would say. "I can still carry myself. If I didn't tell you nobody would have known. But I needed to tell you since I do not know how I would react to the treatment."

During one of those days, she went to the children's schools to see them. She explained to the school authorities that she had to see her children before an urgent trip abroad. They were quite supportive. The children were surprised to see their mother on a day that was not officially their visiting day. She talked at length with the children. Daniella and Davina seemed wary about her reasons for travelling. She assured them that all was well. She told them that their father would be with them when school closed for holidays. She gave them money and provisions. They were overjoyed with the unexpected extras and bid her safe journey.

As the driver pulled away from the school gate, Ofunneka looked back and thought, "What if this is the last time I'm seeing my children?" She almost choked in the bitterness of her own thought. She wept.

She felt the children did not need to know the truth why she was going away. They were too young to carry such a burden. Her brother had told her earlier when she said the children needed not know, that it was part of the reason she was ill. "You carry burdens for yourself and for everyone else," he had told her. "It doesn't make you less of a human being to let your emotions out. It is when you internalize them that they come out in the form of illness." She had responded jokingly saying, "Doctor, teach me. It's a little late now, but if I pull through with this one I would certainly like to change." She knew he spoke the truth. And so they made arrangements. While her brother made preparations for their travel, Ofunneka was making arrangements for her reunion party.

She did some recordings on tape, bought gift items and had them wrapped in small packages with names and other inscriptions written on them. On some of the packages she had written the words 'In case.' No one knew exactly what she was up to, but they let her to do those little things she said she needed to do in peace without questioning. She arranged her house as if she was going on a very long trip.

Enebeli wondered aloud if his sister had not made up her mind about the outcome of her treatment beforehand. Ofunneka had replied, "Only God decides."

Time seemed to crawl like a snail as the true extent of her thoughts began to be made manifest. However, with each passing day, she began to perceive her illness as a life sentence. She wondered why it had to occur when things were near perfect for her. She could not reason with God but she could ask why?

She revived her habit of writing in her journal once more. There she poured out her feelings, the ones she dared not voice out or share with her family, for fear they become despondent. Her jottings were becoming real to her. In one entry she wrote that she felt in a curious way as if she had dropped from the edge of the world but instead of falling downward into an endless pit, she was suspended, dragged by the present in an upstream course towards a point which she could not see. She did not have a say in the matter. She was powerless against its force, utterly at the mercy of the current. If nature was in control, Ofunneka felt no will, no desire to resist. She yielded to its beat, its enormity. In return it brought her relief. It bled the pain she was carrying and sucked away her distress. Its force planted her back into the present, and she remembered her reunion party. It was now imminent and she had to prepare for it.

Chapter 9

The lights in the room seemed to bounce on Ofunneka's gold bedecked neck as she walked slowly to join her friends. They had all agreed to meet here for a party, just the five of them. They had decided on a dress code of black and gold. Ofunneka, ever the fashion queen, chose an exquisite gold and black lace ensemble. The party was at the Crystal Palace, one of the choice private resorts in town. She was the last to get there. As she walked to the table, the others who were already seated and waiting screamed excitedly.

This was the scene she had anticipated. It was the kind of welcome fit for a queen.

She didn't crave for it. She knew the reaction she could elicit from her friends whom she had not seen in more than ten years. She needed such excitement now that she was going through turmoil and pain. She needed it from her good old friends. It made her feel heady and alive. She knew the liveliness from this reunion would help her through the long periods of treatment that would follow. It was good to be in the midst of people who would not make you feel sorrowful. For this reason, she resolved not to tell them. She wanted this reunion to be a happy event without the burden of her pain and their sorrow for her.

They all stood spontaneously as if in honour of a visiting dignitary. It took several minutes of screaming, hugging and backslapping before they settled in their seats.

They had all done well in their various fields. Bola was a practicing lawyer; Ifesinachi, an Accountant who worked in one of the mega banks in town; Mabel, an award-winning investigative journalist from one of the major global news networks. The award was presented to her at a star-studded ceremony in the US and had been in the news for weeks. Halima, was a dealer in expensive jewellery and lace materials which she imported from Europe, and the Middle East. Ofunneka was a fashion designer and owner of a reputable fashion outfit in town. There was one person missing: Funmi, the globetrotter, a high-ranking marketing executive at Andex and Sons. She had died two years earlier in a plane crash on her way from New York to the Netherlands.

The chattering went on non-stop. It was Ofunneka who eventually tried to bring order to the meeting.

"Aren't we forgetting something?" she asked, raising her voice above the excited conversations. "We were supposed to be six here today but we are only five of us around this table." There was dead silence. They all stood up to observe a minute's silence in memory of Funmi. Ofunneka reminded her friends that they had agreed to raise a purse to be given to Funmi's eldest daughter for the upkeep of the children. They raised one million naira on the spot. After that, food and wine flowed as they reminisced on times past.

Ofunneka noticed an unusual tentativeness in Bola's participation. It was as if she was not with them in full.

"Bola, is anything wrong?" she asked. but Bola was not forthcoming. She prodded a little more.

"Look, sister, nothing is worth losing this moment of our lives for. So let's enjoy every bit of it while we still can." With the others also urging Bola to spill it out, tears soon began running down her cheeks.

"My marriage is over!" she cried. Everyone stopped eating. It was as if they lost appetite all at once as an awkward silence descended on the gathering. After what seemed like an eternity, Ifesinachi broke the silence.

"Ofunneka, you should have allowed us finish our meals before prying out Bola's problem.

"Ife-si-na-chi!" Ofunneka retorted, deliberately dragging out her name for emphasis. "Here we are talking about marriage and you are talking about food."

"What's the big deal here? Mine broke years ago. Didn't I tell you? He has even remarried! Why should Bola die because of it? They are only separated. My own is final. I'm not dead because of it."

"We all have different ways of handling disappointment", Ofunneka offered in a conciliatory tone. Then she turned to Bola. "What happened?"

"Where do I begin from? The problem started when I sat down to take stock of our relationship. I realized that I was too eager to marry so I did not take time to ask myself if I could cope with his shortcomings. I did not ask myself if I would be able to handle them for the rest of my life. My parents actually kept drumming it into my ears. I wasn't even happy during courtship because ..."

"Because he was always beating you. He was very jealous, and you thought it was because he loved you," Ifesinachi cuts in.

"Yes, at that time I actually believed it. If he saw me talking with any other man he would beat me. When I saw him with other women, he gave a thousand and one excuses. If I reacted negatively he would still beat me. At one point I didn't know whether I was staying in the marriage because I wanted to or because I was scared of leaving him. A part of me felt that if I left him he would harm me. He would say to me, *Don't ever think of leaving me.* I interpreted it to mean that he loved me beyond words but now I know better."

Ifesinachi interjected. "Thank God your eyes are finally open."

Ofunneka shot her a look as if to say, *Haba! Ifesinachi let her finish.*

"My first miscarriage occurred as a result of his brutality", Bola continued. "Afterwards he would be so sorry. He would be all over me without giving me space to think. He would become so nice that you begin to wonder if it was the same person that was so violent a little while before. This kept happening. Then his finances began to dwindle to the extent that I became the breadwinner of the family. Then the children started coming. I did everything I could to cater for our family. In spite of the moral and financial support that I gave him, he still womanised. Nothing I did pleased him. At a point he made me believe that he was doing me a favour by allowing me bear his name."

"This is ridiculous. Emotional blackmail, that's what that is," Ifesinachi cut in again. This time Mabel who was spellbound by Bola's narrative shouted at her.

"Shut up Ifesinachi!"

The others simply looked at the two of them and gestured Bola to continue.

"At a point I became the husband and wife and I started asking myself what I was doing in the marriage. I felt worthless until I joined the women's group in my church. When I began fasting and praying things picked up a little. I started all night prayers in my house and things became better. At a time my husband began to show interest in such programmes. I began to have hope. Somewhere along the line he developed an interest in one of the female pastors. I was the one who introduced them and they got talking. He became even more serious in Church activities than I. I was happy." At this point, she looked up at her listeners and then continued:

"He would always tell me how pastor advised and counselled him not knowing it was a cover for me not to suspect what was happening between them. You know, as long as no one suspects, murder is easy! I didn't know that Pastor Bose was giving him a reorientation to suit herself. So, right under my nose the supposed changed man was changing for another woman. He came to me one day and said it was out of pressure that he married me. He said he did not want to embarrass me, seeing that we had courted for a very long time. So, to him it was no marriage. It was more of living to the expectations of other people. He told me that he had found his soul mate in Pastor Bose."

"What was your reaction?" Mabel asked, in shock.

"I took the matter to the pastorate of the Church and they called the three of us. After interrogation, they told Pastor Bose to desist from the lure of Satan but Pastor Bose did not care anymore. She said that God revealed to her that Richie, my husband, was her true husband. She added that my marriage to Richie was not contracted in Church but under native law and custom and as far as she was concerned the marriage had not been blessed and as such had not been endorsed by God. Pastor Bose and my husband changed churches and relocated to another community. I do not even know where he is now. My problem is what I am going to tell the children. If he had left us six years ago, I would have been happier but not now." She began to weep all over again.

"Look, let it go," Ofunneka started. "Maybe he wasn't yours in the first place. If he's truly gone, it may be God's will. Let your mind set him free. If he comes back to you he's yours. If not he never was yours. Ask God to give you grace to live without him because as a Christian woman you can't remarry but you can be separated."

"I won't remarry," said Bola.

"Is that so?" Ifesinachi asked. "So, how is my friend, Bola, going to keep warm on cold nights eh? All because she wants to go to heaven."

"You don't question God," Ofunneka said. "As a human being you do what is right and pleasing before Him. We must not take sides. Let judgement be His."

"Have you people finished?" This came from Mabel who had been quiet for some time. "You're crying that a man left you isn't it? He was brutal then he became nice and just when you were about to start reaping the fruit of your labour he left you for another woman. Look at me. I have not even experienced marriage. Where do you want me to begin from? I'm forty years old. None of you here is better behaved than I am. You know that for me it has always been one man at a time. When some of you were jumping from here to there I was steady. I had one relationship for fifteen years but nothing came out of it. He married a wife and had children and I didn't know because I was very trusting."

"You really were a dunce in that relationship," Ifesinachi quipped.

"You may be right. But hear me out and tell me if I was to blame. You see, when I started with him, we were both young. Over the years we promised each other to be together forever. I thought he was keeping his promises like I vowed to keep mine. But no, when he decided to get married he went to his village and got married without my knowing, came back and continued with me as if nothing happened. Automatically, I became the mistress. Each time I broached the subject of marriage, he would say that I should get pregnant first. Unfortunately, I wasn't getting pregnant."

"How impossible can men be?" Bola said.

"I have never misused myself, I have never been pregnant not to talk of having an abortion procedure. I kept wondering why I couldn't get pregnant.

"Maybe he was on pills," Ifesinachi interjected.

"It never occurred to me that a man could be taking pills in order not to impregnate a woman. I thought it was a woman who does, so not the other way round.

"Ifesinachi told you, you were a complete idiot," Bola said.

"No, Bola not from you please. Who is the fool amongst us?"

"Why you dey vex now? No be me talk am. Na Ifesinachi."

"Did Ifesinachi ask you to help her repeat it?"

"See two supposedly smart women, a lawyer and a journalist. See what men can do. Now you want us to vote who is the Dunce between you two," Ifesinachi was the one doing the tongue-lashing now.

Ofunneka couldn't hold her laughter any more. She laughed and nearly fell on the ground. When she regained composure she said to them, "Let me tell you all, we are all idiots when it comes to relationship with men. We are often the ones at the losing end. My father once told me that if I want to remain in my marriage I should become forgiving. He said marriage is for persevering women and any time I dare become impatient I would be walking out of my marriage door and his advice has helped me over the years in my relationship with my husband. Please Mabel, let's hear the end of your ordeal."

"Well, as I was saying before I was rudely interrupted, Richard was so wicked and selfish that when ..."

"Oh, he's no longer Richie eh? He has become Richard?"

"Please, Ifesinachi, let's hear her out. Any more interruption will attract a fifty thousand Naira fine from the culprit," Ofunneka pronounced bringing a near grave silence to the gathering. Mabel continued as if she had not been interrupted in the first instance.

"He was so selfish that when he had finished having the number of children he wanted with his wife he underwent a vasectomy so that whatever he did with me or any woman for that matter would not result in pregnancy. So, I was busy trying to get pregnant while he was busy enjoying the two of us the way he wanted, knowing that nothing could make me get pregnant. I don't know how he managed it or how he did the whole trick but medicine has its peculiarities and I am only concerned with my side of the gist. But then, you must be wondering *How did I get to know*, right?"

"Please tell us. We are dying to know," Bola said.

"Well, I went to a church with him one day and someone who knew him greeted him and asked after his wife and children.

Richard did not respond. When I looked at my Richard, he was stiff like stock fish. So, I asked him: *Do you have a wife and children?* He began to stammer. That was the last thing I heard until I woke up in a hospital. So tell me, where would I begin? Where have I wronged him? I loved him like I never loved anyone before. I trusted him. It was later he explained that he married because of tradition. He needed to keep his royal lineage, that there were specific families he was supposed to marry from in his home town. He said I was the one he loved. I don't understand what people mean when they say they love one person but marry another. What am I supposed to do?"

Halima who had been listening all the while without saying a word now spoke, "Why is it that when changes are to be made in relationships it is the women that would bear the brunt? I mean this love thing should be fifty-fifty, sixty-forty perhaps. Has it ever occurred to you that the number of women in psychiatric hospitals exceeds that of men? And often it is related to heartbreak. Our society does not help in any way. There is no support for women. It's high time we started seminars on issues such as these. Perhaps families should raise their male children to understand that however successful and formidable they are as men, if they have failed marriages then they are altogether failures."

She paused for a while as if waiting for the impact of her words to sink into her listeners.

"How about the bit about changing your name from Esther to Halima. How did that happen?" Ofunneka asked.

"Oh that," Halima said. "Old story. But you people know now. He was brutally handsome. I went weak in the knees when he first approached me. For him to have noticed me at school was a blessing. I didn't want to become a Muslim but the only thing that was keeping him from marrying me was our different faiths. So, I took the offer. What's so terrible about being a Muslim anyway? We all serve the same God. Besides, I was the only one who was a Christian in my family, so it was easy for me to change. I did it to show him how much I loved him. But I didn't think of the polygamous aspect of his religion. We were educated. We had a good relationship so he wouldn't want another wife if I was giving him what he needed. I felt he would settle for a monogamous life but I was wrong. Five years into the marriage, he wanted another wife. I didn't believe it. As I speak to you now, we're three. He and I live in the main house. The other wives live within the same complex. You've been to my house, Bola. We're all having children here and there as if it's a competition. Do you know how it is? You're talking about mistresses. The mistress could see you and hide or your husband would conceal the relationship. Nobody conceals this one. We all know when our man is sleeping with our rivals. I think our problem as women is that we dream too much. As a Muslim woman, I should have expected that my husband would want to marry more women and prepared myself for it. The men are not the only ones to blame. Women are their own worst enemies. Men are voracious when it comes to women but it takes another woman for a man to cheat."

"Oh yes, tell them!" Ifesinachi hailed. "Say it sister! I feel you!"

"It's amazing that women date married men but when they get married they want to kill any other woman they see near their husbands. It is a vicious circle. I didn't have an affair with another woman's husband. My husband and I started going out as singles. Now, what am I supposed to do when another woman agrees to marry him knowing that he already has a wife?

"You won't believe this: when he went for the third, the second wife actually hit the roof! I remember what my parents used to say; 'What happens in the house of a goat will eventually happen in the house of the chicken.' All of a sudden, she wanted to align with me so that we could deal with the third wife. I just wasn't interested. It was good for her to feel how I felt when my husband brought her in. The third wife is feeling like the main dish now. Her time will elapse. We are really our own enemies."

"Good point," Ofunneka contributed, almost like a moderator – a role she seemed to be increasingly playing in their discussion for the night. "I agree that we are our own enemies. We allow the men have their way either because of abject poverty or because we feel incomplete without them."

"Adviser, what about you? Tell us your own story. Or are we the only ones with men who stray?" That was Bola addressing Ofunneka.

"My story is too long."

"Ehee, cut it short and tell us," they all chorused.

"I'll tell you.

"What is going on in your life," Mabel asked.

"What is going on is that I am going on a trip. I have a programme. I need to run my master's programme in cognitive behavioural therapy."

"You're already a born counsellor," someone quipped.

"I want to be certified. That's what I want to do next."

Bola said, "Eheh! What about your husband and children, who will take care of them in your absence?"

"The children are grown up now. It's just for nine months. They should be able to take care of themselves till I come back."

"Really?" Bola said, "I wish I had that kind of understanding with my husband."

She said she was going to join her husband in the US in a few days.

"Aha! So we're lucky to have seen you eh?" Halima asked.

"I guess you could say I'm lucky to have seen you all on my way out of the country."

"Please try and keep in touch," Halima said.

"And buy some presents when you're coming back," Bola added.

Soon, they started talking about their children. "I don't think we behaved the way our children are behaving now", Bola said. "I still remember that if my mother told me to jump, my response was usually *How high?* Nowadays, when you tell your children to jump, the response you get is, *Why?*" They all laughed cheerily at this.

Bola continued, "When you tell your child anything or send him or her on an errand, you would need to explain why. I don't get it. The girls will tell you that you're now old school. What is this old school thing about? When you want to put them in shape morally they tell you that you're old school."

They became so engrossed in the chatter and fun they were having in each other's company. Ofunneka excused herself to go to the ladies. As she walked away, she told herself, "I won't look back. I hope I'm not seeing my friends for the last time. God, please give me the chance to come back and explain to them why I left like this."

As the car drove away, she was asking herself, "Was it the right way to leave? Should I have explained to them what I'm going through? If I don't live through this, would they understand why I left the way I did?" She made a mental note that when she got home she would write to the four of them explaining the reason for her leaving without saying goodbye. She would hand it over to her brother with instructions to send it to them if she dies. If she survives, she would personally go to each of their homes to explain. She was already on the expressway when Bola noticed.

"How long does it take Ofunneka to ease herself?" She stormed to the ladies. As she opened the door, she called out, "Girl! Girl!!." The place was empty. She went back to inform the others that Ofunneka had vanished.

Ifesinachi was angry. "What? I don't know what is wrong with Ofunneka. She came in last and she is the first to go. She didn't even have the courtesy to tell us."

Bola asked her to calm down. "There is something unusual in this behaviour of Ofunneka," she said. "Did you notice she wasn't really her lively self all through the time she was here? Perhaps a call came in and she had to run."

"Even if there was an emergency, she should have told us" Ifesinachi said. She dialled her phone. "You see, she has even switched off her phone. Who in God's name does things like that?"

"No please," Halima pleaded. "Let's not end today like this. Though Ofunneka has left, let us still go and do what we've agreed to do for Funmi's children. Let us agree on a convenient time and place to meet and hand over the money to her first daughter. It is important that the children know that we didn't forget them."

They agreed that even if all of them did not come, Halima should take the money to the children. But Halima said that all the five of them should come together and do it. Ifesinachi corrected, "Now we are four."

"So, let the four of us come together and do it," Halima persisted.

They were still arguing about the matter when a call came through. Halima's husband wanted her home. He said something urgent had come up. "He hasn't interrupted me like this before. He knows I came for this reunion and he knows we've not seen each other for over ten years. Something must have happened." She excused herself. "We'll talk tomorrow girls," she said as she blew kisses at them and rushed to the foyer. The others stood up. They talked as they walked to their chauffeured cars.

Halima's husband could afford to have a guest house in Lagos though they lived in Kaduna. He had numerous business concerns in Lagos. Halima had come to Lagos because of the reunion with her friends. It had coincided with her husband's business meeting, or so Halima had thought. They had come together to Lagos a few days earlier. There had been no sign of any problem when she left their guest house for the reunion party around six p.m

She wondered what was so urgent that couldn't wait for her to enjoy the company of her friends, as the car sped down the Third Mainland Bridge back to the Government Reserved Area (GRA) Ikeja where their guest house was. She was so uncertain and already fretting by the time the driver packed the car in the garage. She got off and quickened her steps. She opened a sliding door to reveal a very opulent sitting room.

Her husband was seated as she entered. He got up and came towards her in welcome with a broad smile on his face. She thought, "Oh, maybe he won a contract and can't wait to share the good news with me.'

"If it's good news why couldn't it wait? You know I haven't seen my friends in years."

"I know, I know, you know you're my first wife. Issues like this I should tell you ahead of others."

"What is so wonderful?" she asked.

"Sit down my wife. You've been very good, taking care of all your younger wives and you know, to reduce the burden on you I thought I should complete the number."

"What is that? Complete what number? I don't understand?"

"At least sit down first. It is very good news. I come to Lagos often and most times this house feels too big and empty. I cannot take one of you with me each time I come to Lagos."

"We have not complained yet. Am I not here with you now? Sekira can come. Hanatu can come. Has any of us refused to follow you to Lagos or anywhere before?"

"I'm not making excuses to you," he said. "What I'm saying is that I need a family here. What is wrong with that? I'm not saying…"

"What is not wrong with that?" She was already very angry and could not control it.

"What is annoying you?" her husband asked surprised at her response.

"Oh! So, all these years it has not occurred to you that these things hurt. I'm co-wife with how many women? We don't even have enough of you to share, now you're adding number four? Where does that leave me? I'm just there watching them, acting mother hen. I no longer understand. I am glad though that Hanatu now knows how it feels not to be the star."

"Please lower your voice, she's already here," he said.

"You mean she's already here?"

"Yes, I told her to come and pay homage."

"Homage to who? An empty queen? Please do not mock me. There's no need for that." And she stomped out.

"I'm talking to you and you're walking out on me, don't push me to say things I shouldn't say to you. A woman should be respectful to her husband."

She came back to the living room. "Who is not respecting you now? Why are you looking for respect again from me." As she was still talking, lo and behold a very young and pretty girl of about nineteen years stepped into the living room. Halima looked at her not knowing what to say. In a reflex action, she turned away. The girl knelt and greeted her. All Halima could think of was, "If only she knows what she's getting into." She turned and acknowledged the girl's greeting and asked, "Is she the one?"

"Yes", Alhaji replied. He made a sign for the girl to leave.

Halima waited a few seconds as the girl excused herself. Then she said to him, "She's only a child."

"Who told you?" Alhaji asked. "How old were you when I married you? You were older than her by just a few years. She's the one. She will be living here in Lagos."

Halima sat and stared into space. Alhaji asked if she was all right. She replied, "This is too much to take in one night. You've always done what pleased you. You did not need my consent. There was no need for this introduction. I need a rest. I have a busy day tomorrow. My friends and I are going to visit Funmi's daughter. You remember Funmi, my friend who died two years ago. I am the closest to the children so I have to be there. You should remember when they were living in Kaduna they used to visit us."

"Oh," said her husband. "We are discussing family matters here and you're bringing your friends into it. I can see your friends are more important to you."

"Which family matter? Did you discuss the issue with me before you went ahead and married your number four? Oh, I should abandon my commitment and the reason why I came to Lagos in the first place because of *mata* number four?"

Alhaji started to grumble. "You women are so impossible, if I did not show you respect as senior wife you would have complained. Now I have done so and you are not satisfied." He left her in the sitting room staring into space, surprised that he expected her to be happy and be reasonable. After a while, she went to bed. She couldn't sleep. The giant seven foot bed that was usually too big even for two people was suddenly too small for her. The beautifully furnished room she used to love sleeping in became an empty space. The large wall mirror became just a frame. Her interest in everything waned. In her mind she kept asking, "Can I take this? How much longer can I endure this?" She wept.

Her mind went to Ofunneka. She remembered their conversations the few times they spoke on phone over the years. Ofunneka had said to her, "When you feel unworthy and you think you're no longer important, if you let people make you feel less, whether husband or children, friends or neighbours, it is because you allowed them." She thought to herself, "Since I'm no longer important to him, I think I should generate happiness for myself."

She then made up her mind that instead of brooding or crying over broken eggs, she would, as soon as she got back to Kaduna start investing more of her time in her business, taking better care of her children and discovering anew who she really is. She would find new things she really wanted to do. If he came to her, fine, if he didn't fine. What you share can never be enough. A fool at forty they say is a fool forever. She did not want to be a fool forever. She couldn't make a fresh start but she could manage what was left of her time well and be useful to herself and those who needed her.

She wondered why she was crying. The answer almost came to her mind immediately: *Because I just buried the old me. This is a new me. The new me is going to participate more actively in my community. I will find young girls who are willing to go to school and put them through school and be their mentor.*

She was already doing that before but this time she was going to go further. She planned to generate income from other sources for the venture. She knew a few people who could support her. Her husband's friends were very rich. Her dream had always been to establish an NGO that would cater for the less privileged in society. She was going to do just that; she was going to learn to follow her dreams. As she contemplated these thoughts she found that she was at peace. She slept off.

The next morning, she was in high spirits. She got dressed, and as she stepped out of her room she noticed that the new wife was already up and about. Her first thought was, "You were the one that slept with him." But she quickly controlled the flow of her thoughts and cautioned herself, "I want to be the one to control my thoughts, not my thoughts controlling me. I don't want to know what they did last night," She thought within her

She met Rekiya the new wife in the living room, cleaning and arranging furniture. Rekiya greeted her and she responded cheerfully.

"How are you? Did you sleep well?" she asked.

"Yes," came the reply.

Why wouldn't you sleep well? She thought as she flashed a smile at Rekiya then said, "Good, I'm on my way out. You know where the kitchen is. Prepare something for yourself and Alhaji for breakfast.

This is your home now. We are actually your guests here."

When she stepped out onto the frontage, she beckoned to the driver who was sitting by the gate and spoke a few words to him. He ran and brought out her car from the garage. They drove off.

As she was being driven away, she thought, *By the time he comes out he would realize I have gone out. I must not give him the satisfaction of knowing that I'm jealous. This is what he would never see again.* She made calls and made the necessary arrangements with her friends for their visit. She gave them the address and they agreed to meet at the place at an agreed time. When they got there, Funmi's eldest daughter, Serena, was overwhelmed to the point of tears.

"I thought you'd forgotten us, Auntie Halima," she said amidst tears.

"No I didn't."

"You were at the burial and after that I didn't see you again. I know you call and send things to us. I didn't know how to tell you we needed more than the things you sent."

"It's okay," replied Halima. "I will come more often now. How are your younger ones? Where are they?"

"They are in school. I'm at home because I just came back from the NYSC camp."

Halima signalled to her friends who joined them. When Serena saw them she was ecstatic and rushed towards them to welcome them. They commented on how big a girl she had become. They asked how she recognized them. She told them that her mother used to point them out to her one by one in pictures. She called each of them by their names, "Auntie Bola, Auntie Mabel, Auntie Ifesinachi." Then she asked, "What about the other aunty that always dressed like a girl?"

"Oh, Ofunneka," Ifesinachi said sharply. "It's a story for another day. Just leave her out of it. I don't want anybody to spoil my mood today."

"Ifesinachi!" Bola exclaimed.

"No, don't call me oh!" Ifesinachi snapped back. "Let's not go back to that disappearing act she did yesterday." They all looked at her and shook their heads. When they were seated in the living room, Halima said to Serena, "You're the Ada of the family ..."

Serena asked what Ada meant. Ifesinachi explained that being the eldest child and a girl entitled her to be called Ada.

Halima continued, "So, as the eldest daughter of your mother, you must let her live in you. When you carry her name very well it means she didn't die. She ascended. There's continuity."

Serena said she knew and did not intend to forget or embarrass her mother. Her only regret was that her mother had unfulfilled dreams. That was why her mother always told her that no matter what happens she should follow her dreams. She must recognize that how you present yourself determines how you are perceived."
"It is so my dear, your mother taught you well", Bola said.

"It's not as if your mother's dreams were unfulfilled. She let her dreams go in order for you to attain yours. As a mother, you sometimes step aside so your children can spring forth. It doesn't make you less. Certain things must die for others to grow. They become the manure that nourishes the others. Your mother didn't quite finish school. She suspended it when she got married and children started coming. She had to take care of the home while your father continued his education because there was really not enough money for the two of them to continue their education. Your father had to travel abroad at some point after they had all of you, in pursuit of a higher degree. It was assumed that his improvement in education would better the lot of the family. But he never came back. So, your mother was saddled with the sole responsibility of raising you and your younger ones; to give you a good start in life. Even whilst doing that, she struggled to improve herself. She enrolled for the National Certificate in Education, NCE, and finished it. Though she had wanted to be a doctor, she opted for the NCE programme because it afforded her the opportunity of working and attending school."

"Yes, my mother was a strong woman who made tremendous sacrifices for us. I will always remember her for that."

"Remember her also for the fact that despite obstacles and bringing up four children single-handedly, she made tremendous improvements personally. She had her Bachelor in Education degree, B. Ed, and went on to become a principal. Being a principal is the peak you get to as a teacher and she attained that before she turned forty. The feat was almost unheard of. God did compensate her. She had rapid promotions. Look at all of you her children; you're all well brought up. If only she had spent more time at Andex and Sons, she could have done greater things."

"Unfortunately," said Serena, "mother insisted that we bear our father's name. This is a man I can barely remember, who did not contribute anything to my upbringing."

"No, Serena, your mother was right. After all, you are your father's child. You can't be anyone else." Halima said. "And to be fair to your father's family, they rallied round you people. They were always supportive. Well it was because your mother was a good woman. Your father never bothered about you and eventually when he did come home, he came with an *oyinbo* – a foreign wife – and two kids. Your parents had a good relationship. It's just that they lost contact and drifted apart."

"It was my father who wanted it that way! It was as if to him we never existed. I just never understood it. At a time I wanted my mother to remarry but she never wanted to. She was too busy being a mother to really care about her own happiness. So, I sometimes feel she didn't enjoy life. I resolved that when I finish youth service, I will get a job first before I even think of a relationship. All the mistakes she made, by the grace of God I won't make them."

"There's no guaranty in any relationship. It takes the grace of God to make them work. If you're watchful there are signs that will lead you right but the problem is that most women refuse to see those signs even when they stare them in the face. It's not as if we are not aware of these signs but usually we choose to see what we want to see and hear what we want to hear especially when we are blinded by love. I would advise you to be very watchful and carry your mother's name well."

"Thank you, Auntie Ifesinachi, I will."

Halima handed her the money they had brought. She said, "This is a token from your mother's five good friends. You should use it wisely for the upkeep of your younger ones and yourself especially in your siblings' educational pursuits. We will leave our phone numbers for you in case in future you'll need any help. You should not hesitate to call any of us. It is important that there is continuity."

"It is also important that you should learn to accept whatever has happened as the will of God and learn to forgive your father, no matter how painful it is. I think even at your young age you're coping very well," Ifesinachi said.

"What else will I do? My mother is gone. I cannot bring her back no matter what I do or how long I mourn her. I leave everything to God."

"That's well said," Mabel responded.

They all hugged her and prayed for her and her younger ones, then got up to leave. Outside, where they parked their cars, Ifesinachi turned to Halima and asked, "You've not told us what was so urgent that your husband wanted you home, was it another honeymoon?"

Halima stopped, looked up to the skies and shook her head. They quickly dismissed Serena who thanked them again and again and went back in. They stood together and Halima said, "You will not believe it, wife number four has arrived." They all screamed.

Ifesinachi said, "It's you people that are allowing this nonsense. Well, as I always say, in life the choice lies solely with you. If you choose to be happy you'd be. If you choose to be sad, you'll equally be. You go ahead, find those things that will make you happy and do them but let them be things that are right. "I've considered many things," Halima said. "I've made up my mind about setting up an NGO. I want to step out of myself and make a difference in other people's lives because that makes me happy."

"That's the spirit sister," Bola enthused. "I too have decided to be more committed to church activities. I will look for women who are like-minded who want to improve themselves spiritually rather than comparing jewelleries and apparels."

"Halima," Mabel the quiet one began. "Do not go eating yourself up because you have too many people to share your apple with. Let's go back to our various homes, take care of our children, take care of our men and most importantly take care of ourselves because it's when you're fit that you can take care of others. I will always pray that this friendship should continue. May God surround us with people who want to draw us closer to Him and who would help us fulfil our dreams."

They hugged and promised to keep in touch more often and departed after a most wonderful evening.

Chapter 10

It was the first week of November and signs of yuletide were already everywhere. Ofunneka, her mother and husband were under a fountain. Ofunneka got up and paced. Her steps were controlled and steady but she felt like a caged cat. Amah joined her as she stopped under a shade beneath an alcove. The rush of water from the fountain and an occasional splash from a brook below were the only sounds that could be heard. Amah enveloped her in a tight hug from behind.

"I don't want to lose you," he said.

"You're not losing me," she replied and giggled.

Otua, who was close by, heard what was being said and reacted.

"I shouldn't be hearing such words from any of you," She got up to leave.

"Mama, wait," Ofunneka said lightly. "Things happen not because the people they happen to deserve them. Look at Enebeli your son, my brother. Look at who he's turned out to be in spite of the circumstances of his birth. One may live to take care of one's children and they may not turn out right. Another may be dead and God in his infinite mercy would place the children in the care of people that would bring them up right. Given the choice I would love to be alive to raise my children the way you raised me. Okay, look at it this way: You were the sickly one between you and dad, but you're the one who is alive today and father who was always strong is dead. How did he die? It was just in a space of thirty seconds. He cried his chest, his chest, broke out in sweat and he was gone. But you who have been in and out of hospital are here. It's all been destined."

"This is different. It is not my destiny to bury my child. I reject that."

"Yes, we are praying that I do not die before you. But I'm not the only one you have now. Aren't you lucky you have grandchildren? If I had died years ago wouldn't you have taken care of them? From my history nobody thought I would be here today. Having six children is not a joke. The youngest is almost a teenager. There are people who never had children and some people who never even got married. We've had our ups and downs..."

She looked at her husband who cut in, "I regret the ups and downs. I wish we had tried harder to be happy together. I wonder why it has taken a sad turn of events for us to come to our senses."

He turned to Enebeli who had just joined them and was yet to catch the drift of their conversation.

"Enebeli, please don't waste your marital years competing with your wife or trying to prove how much of a man you are, by sleeping around with other women. You don't have to. As you get older, you begin to realise that extra marital affairs are not necessary. By then, you may have destroyed your home. See what is happening now... God forbid, but if something terrible happens to Ofunneka, where will I begin from? Temptations come quite alright but a man should have the will to say no to what is wrong. You see, I had a friend who made it quite clear in those days that I couldn't come to his office or his home with a mistress. I disliked him so much because I felt he was acting holier than thou..."

"You mean there are still men like that?" Ofunneka interjected.

"Of course," Amah said. "Tunji and Abel were two in a million. I never saw their type. I can say that Tunji never cheated on his wife. He used to tell me, *What I wouldn't want her to do to me I wouldn't do to her*. At the close of work each day, he would go straight back home. He took care of his children. He would bathe them. They would have dinner together every evening. So, each time he started talking I would just look at him and smile. *Holy* nweje, I used to call him. And really, he did not miss out on any fun we thought we were having. Once he felt the spark was going off his marriage he would go for a reunion with his wife. He called it *re-launch*. They would travel to somewhere exotic, do something different. He used to ask me, *What is it that you're looking for in these girls?* Sometimes my excuse would be that I wanted to make a difference in their lives by helping them. Some of them were very poor, I put them through school. But when I checked myself, I really didn't get true satisfaction."

"So, why do it when there's no satisfaction?" Enebeli asked.

"My other excuse used to be that the home is noisy with children running up and down. When you come home you see your wife looking harassed and not as elegant as you would want. By contrast, there's a certain serenity you get outside your home in a single woman's house. These girls massage your feet. They go the extra mile to be presentable and to please you. That's something most married women stop doing once they have the ring on their fingers."

"It's nothing but a negation of your marriage vows," Ofunneka said.

"Yes. Many men who indulge in this know that but sometimes they can't help themselves. My friend Tunji was so against it that he would ask what the girls are doing that your wife can't do for you. He would say if there is, tell your wife to do it and she would gladly do it for you. Have you told her and she refused? He would often ask and my answer was usually no, and frankly I didn't tell Ofunneka. The few times I had guts to ask, she did more than I requested." He turned to Ofunneka and said, "I know I've caused you pain with my indiscretions. And I've asked for forgiveness in the past. I want to know, am I really forgiven?"

"It took a while to forgive. But I eventually really forgave you. To forget is a different kettle of fish! The most difficult to erase from my mind was when you got involved with someone I called my friend and accepted into our home. Unknown to me, you were in a sizzling relationship with her. It was a monumental betrayal! There were other instances that were really bad but each time I remembered that I vowed for better for worse. There was a time I prayed for those girlfriends of yours to get married to unfaithful husbands so that they would feel my pain..."

At this point Otua and Enebeli walked to another part of the fountain, leaving the couple alone.

"That was my prayer for them. Those girls usually thought, *After all, he takes care of his wife and children; I do not deprive them.* But there's more to being a husband than just being a breadwinner. Every wife wants her husband to herself. When I grew in the Lord I changed my prayer for them. I started asking God to give them their own husbands so that they would leave mine for me. I prayed that they should see the light and understand that what they did was wrong."

Amah pleaded that they should not dwell much on past mistakes. He said, "Sometimes we men know there's no excuse for extra-marital affairs but we look for excuses to do it."

"Wait. Let me tell you one more," Ofunneka said. "I know it's been a long time but try and remember one trip we had. We went for a weekend at Obudu Cattle Ranch and we had so much fun in each other's company. It was like igniting the flames of love once again. We returned home on a Monday and two days later you packed your bags and said you were going for a conference. You forgot we had the extension line to the phone in our bedroom and I overheard your conversation. It was actually the call from a girl that woke me up. I overhead you say to her that your wife was sleeping and that you were on your way. You told her not to worry that this trip is for her and that you'll see her soon. So, I came down and made so much fuss about your travelling. I insisted you were not going anywhere. You were frantic. You were angry. There was nothing you didn't say but because I knew it was not a business trip I put my foot down. I seized your bag and you slapped me because you wanted to spend time with your girlfriend. In the end, your trip with the girl was put off because of my insistence and she had the guts to call you while I was listening to say, *Sweetheart, I know you want so much to spend the time with me but that bitch of a wife is not allowing you to come, and I know you're so miserable there now.* So, I told her over the extension, *If you're that confident that he loves you tell him to marry you. And, by the way, the 'bitch' is your mother, not me. If you were properly brought up by your mother you wouldn't be running after married men to rescue you from abject poverty.*" She paused for a while at this point. Took in a deep breath, then continued: "I felt really good after saying that. You were so shocked at my response you couldn't even drop the phone, I walked up to you with the phone still in your hands, remember?"

She paused for a while as if in thought, then said, "I miss them." He looked at her wondering who she was referring to, not following her trail. "I mean our children, I don't know if it was right not to tell them what I'm going through. Was I right in trying to protect them?"

"It's okay. Let it be as it is. Since your brother and mother would be here with you I'll travel back home and be with them. Let them think you've actually gone to do a course. That's what you really want, isn't it?"

"Yes, it is but I would like Mama to go back to Nigeria after one month."

Mama protested her suggestion when she was told.

"Yes mama, I would want you to go back. I want you to look inside of yourself and ask, *Apart from Ofunneka, who else do I have?* You have yourself. You have Enebeli. You have your grandchildren. If anything happens to me today and you maintain this idea that I am the only one you have, what will become of you?"

"You're sounding like your father to me now," Otua said.

"Well, that's the truth. When papa died you went to pieces. That was understandable considering that you lost a precious husband suddenly. But I think one should learn to move on and to keep the memories of loved ones alive in a positive way. Each time we talk we say 'papa would have said or done this.' It means he's alive in us. That's the way it should be. I believe that you learnt a lot from papa."

"Of course I did," Otua replied.

"Then, this is the time to show it. If you're not strong what do you want me to do? Mothering is not living your life for your child but letting your child be and having the confidence that the child will survive. You taught me that much. Why do you think that I am distancing myself from my children at this time? It is not because I think I will not leave here alive but because I want them to start imbibing the reality that with or without me they would still survive."

"I am hungry," Enebeli announced, drawing laughter from everyone. They made plans to go out for dinner but Ofunneka wouldn't go because her mind was occupied and she didn't want them to notice how unsettled she was. After dinner, they retired. For the first time in her marital life, without any grudge or ill feeling, she told her husband she wanted to sleep alone. This only happened when they had a quarrel. He couldn't understand it this time but she insisted.

"Yes, I do want to sleep alone and please get use to it. When we get back to Nigeria I would like to be sleeping in my own room. We do not need to prove anything. We could be separate and be the same."

He didn't find it funny but he agreed so as to please her. She told him that the adjoining room was his but if he felt like being with her in the middle of the night he could crossover.

At night she tossed and turned on her bed. So did her husband. He had always wanted them to have separate rooms but she had never wanted that. She reasoned that at the close of the day if they had issues to sort out in the course of turning and tossing, it could trigger reconciliation. *It is easier to reconcile when you share your bed, it reduces the strain and duration of marital quarrels*, she always thought.

This particular night she realised that there were certain decisions she was making that she had no control over. She didn't know whether it's her brain or her heart that was in control but she kept feeling that what she was doing was right and so, she kept making certain arrangements. She made calls, she was asking for things.

Her husband didn't like what was happening but she was in such a realm that nobody could understand, not even herself. She had so much confidence that all was well. She kept on like this till the D-day arrived.

She took her shot of intravenous chemotherapy. It was quite an unnerving experience. It was terrible for her. She could not explain how she felt. She was nauseated, spat and vomited. It took about three days for her to be able to take a cup of tea. She remembered when, years back, while taking her bath she saw a reddish spot on her right breast. As she pressed the spot she felt a sharp pain and at the same time pus came out and she could see inside the opening. She felt there was no problem then. She thought it was only when you feel a lump and there's no pain that you should ask for help. Boils everywhere used to plague her. She felt that the boils had now affected her breast. So, she never took it seriously. Perhaps if she had taken time to go to the hospital for examination this would have been prevented.

Enebeli was supportive during those days when she was depressed before the effect of treatment wore off. After three to four days she could sit up, take some cereal and converse a while. By the time she went for the fourth regimen, she had lost weight, and her hair was falling off but she was in good spirit. She started wearing a wig. She tried to go out with Enebeli and Iza once in a while to the supermarket. Enebeli marvelled at her resilience and often wondered to himself 'what was the thing that could bring his sister down. He could not withstand the trauma she was going through but she still found the strength to do things in spite of herself.

She strained to call her children. She told them not to call, that she would be the one to call. She told them that she was very busy with classes and studies and wouldn't want their calls to interfere. Whenever she mustered enough strength to put a call through, she pretended to be excited so they would not suspect what she was going through.

Her brother called her an 'award-winning actress.' Iza her sister in-law once said to Enebeli, "I've never seen a woman with her strength. We do the crying. At worst, tears would run down her cheeks and she wouldn't even want anyone to see them."

There were arrangements Ofunneka was making that they could not understand. There were parcels she arranged in a box and placed a 'special' tag on and mandated them not to open unless something happened. At the end of six months she came to the close of her treatment. There was hope. The doctors gave her a clean bill of health and said she could be discharged within a month. She decided to use whatever was left of her energy to enrol and complete a crash programme for six weeks so it would not be a total lie she told her children.

She put a call through to her husband who arrived within days. They travelled back to Nigeria and to their family. The children were ecstatic on her arrival but they commented about her weight loss. It was Amah who covered up for her when he said, "You know your mother had always wanted to slim down. She went to US and burned all the fat. Doesn't she look better now?" he asked them smiling.

They agreed with him that their mother looked better in her near slim frame. The reunion with her family was great and everything went well. She couldn't stop thanking God for his mercies.

Chapter 11

O funneka shuffled out of bed with a broad smile across her face. Her father's words still echoed in her mind, like it had happened in reality. She had had a long discussion with her father in a dream that had been soothing and enlightening. She walked to the bathroom and indulged in a long bath as she sang. After this, she got her phone and sent e-mails to her friends telling them why she had left them at the reunion party in the way she did. She told them that she had actually been ill but did not want to be burdened with their anticipated sympathy which led to her withholding the information from them. Though time had passed, she knew that it was the right thing to do.

They all visited and her conversations with them, though on different days and in different visits was almost identical, like something read from a novel.

"Ofunneka, how would you keep such a thing from us?"

"Like I told you in the email, I didn't want to burden you with my illness. There are too many other burdens and loads in the world that we all carry."

"How would you say such a thing? What are friends for, if not to share burdens and joys? Plus, who told you that you are a burden? We [*or I, depending on the person*] are always here for you. Don't you dare ever keep such a thing from us again, okay?"

Then she would share some of her struggles, plans for the future before they branched into a different topic.

Each prayed with her, thanked God for her recovery and asked for many more years of good health ahead. She also found strength to let her children into the secret. It was tough on them but as a family, they grew strong for each other to get better.

In the following years, Ofunneka found so much joy as things blossomed bringing so much joy to her. Her last child, Ossai, graduated from secondary school and announced to the family that he wanted to train as a chef. He became the butt of countless jokes thereafter. Some said after all the money spent on sending him to school all he wanted to do was cook.

"That doesn't require special training," started Tunji, one of their family friends, "Our mothers never went to school to learn to cook, yet they cooked great meals."

The people around had laughed but Ossai did not find the comment funny. He was firmly resolved. He announced to anyone who would listen that after his degree, he would own the greatest restaurant in the world. Ofunneka regarded everything calmly and with a smile. She helped Ossai scout online for a good school. Although the family policy had been for each of the children to earn their first degrees in Nigeria before going abroad for further studies, they were willing to make an exception for Ossai because now Ofunneka had lots of relatives and friends who could look after him there.

Next came her eldest daughter's wedding. After months of fervent preparation, it was time. The traditional and church wedding ceremonies were colourful with relations and friends coming from different places, almost outdoing themselves as they gave gifts. Ofunneka was overwhelmed at the show of love and smiled all through the events. She wished the wedding could go on forever but it was over soon and life continued. Friends and relatives started calling her *Potential Grandmother*. It was a prospect she was excited at. Several times, she had to pinch herself to ascertain it was all real. It was as if she was in a trance. This was one of the favours she had asked of God during the long nightmare of her illness. Now that it came to pass, she was numb with excitement. As if in answer to their hailing which Ofunneka took as a prayer, her daughter called her to say she was pregnant. Ofunneka was excited beyond words. She danced with Amah, her husband and they felt their love rekindled.

One night, she came into Amah's room and lay beside him. For some strange reason, she decided she did not want to sleep in her room. He was pleasantly surprised and smiled like a child who had been given a new toy. After some time, he nudged her.

"What is it?" she asked, she knew he had a favour to ask. He smiled.

"Eh…Darling, can you, eh, please give me a massage?" he said and winked.

"Don't you know I'm a potential grandmother? Grandmas don't do massage," she teased as she opened her eyes in mock horror. They both laughed as she got up. She tapped him on the buttocks, and slowly let her hands massage him, forming her hands into small fists as she hit him softly at various points.

"Thank you," Amah said, with a large smile that expressed his satisfaction. After a few seconds, his smile was replaced with a frown. "Darling, you look tired."

"Hmmm. It is true o. I don't know why but I feel very weak and tired."

"Well, then rest for a while."

She nodded and lay on the bed.

"My feet are feeling cold," she said in a barely audible whisper.

Amah switched off the air conditioner in the room, took a jar of ointment, sat beside her and massaged her feet. When she felt better, he got a pair of stockings and wore them on her feet. She smiled as he stroked her hair, then he said: "I don't want to disturb you, let me go to the living room and watch the football match on television."

"By all means please do and thank you very much," she replied.

He kissed her and went to the living room. At the end of the match, he came back to the room bubbling with excitement.

"We won! We won!" he shouted. No response. He moved closer to the bed. "Ofunneka, I said we won." No response still. He reasoned that she was still fast asleep and decided not to wake her up. But when he put on the room light to look for something in the wardrobe, he noticed that her neck was tilted at an awkward angle. He went to adjust her neck and felt her body, cold.

He began to shake her but there was no response from the now lifeless body. He shook her more rigorously, not knowing what else to do. All he wanted was for her to open her eyes and talk to him. As realization dawned on him, he began to scream.

"No! No! No! It can't be true! No! No! No! This can't be true! She spoke to me not quite an hour ago! She said thank you! Thank you for what? Is that all you have to say? Ofunneka, wake up! I can't do this alone! No, not after what we've been through. You fought breast cancer and survived. This is the best time of our lives and now you're ... no, you can't do this! No! Wouldn't you wait to see our grandchildren? What do you want me to tell them?"

He screamed on for a few minutes then suddenly became quiet. Almost like a robot, he arranged her properly. He straightened her body so she could remain beautiful. He removed the socks making sure no part of her was bent. Then he looked at her, intently.

"Ah, my beautiful Ofunneka, what will I do now? Lord I don't have her faith. I'm just learning how to be a man in the real sense of the word. All my vows you don't want me to see through...

What do you want me to do? She's only Fifty-five! What do you want me to tell your mother? What do I tell your children? What do I tell our children? Ofunneka, what do you want me to do now?" He stood there asking questions, talking to himself, not knowing what to do. "No! No! No!" he screamed again, then took a hand to his mouth as he sobbed. He lay beside her, his head resting on her chest. He remained in that position with tears slowly cascading his face and wetting her body.

If you love me, then you must pull yourself together and get over your grief quickly. You must survive to keep me alive.

He raised his head up with a start and looked at Ofunneka. He could have sworn he heard her speak those words but she was as still as she had been since he discovered she was dead. He rubbed his eyes to be sure he was not going mad. Then it dawned on him that he had to alert someone at least. He looked at her again and shook her, to no avail. He reached for his phone and scrolled through his phonebook for Enebeli's number, then pressed the 'Dial' icon.

"Is your wife there?" he asked as soon as he heard the croaky *Hello* from the other end.

"Yes, of course," Enebeli replied "How's my sister?"

"Sit down."

"I am sitting down. Why are you telling me to sit down?"

"I'm telling you to sit because of what I have to say to you."

"What is it?" Enebeli sprang to his feet without thinking.

"Ofunneka just left us," Amah said in a calm voice, and then began to sob. Silence followed, then he heard the phone drop at the other end of the connection.

He called his best friend, Eze. Then he made a series of other calls to close relatives on both sides of the family. He was on one of those calls when his eyes fell on a small box in the open wardrobe. It was labelled "Special & Fragile" in Ofunneka's unmistakable handwriting. He had seen it before but never got to ask her what was inside. Now, he opened the box and found a letter addressed to him. His hands shaking, he tore the sealed envelope open. At that moment, he heard a knock on the front door. He dropped the letter and went to answer the door. It was his friend Eze whom he had called earlier. Amah broke down again in tears as he narrated to Eze the circumstances of Ofunneka's demise.

Soon, other people began to arrive. They took Ofunneka's body to the mortuary. Amah fell into cold silence. He would not talk to anyone. Everybody tried to console him but it is hard to calm the rivers of grief flowing from a man who has lost the sun of his life. When Ofunneka's mother was informed of her death, she lost touch with reality. She talked non-stop and had to be sedated. She remained under medication throughout the funeral ceremonies. Now and then, tears rolled down Amah's cheeks. On one of those days following her demise, he suddenly remembered the letter. He rushed to the wardrobe where he had dropped the letter. He opened it desperately like a parched weary traveller in the desert trying to open a bottle of water.

If you are reading this, then I am really dead, the letter began

He sat there, shoulders slumped, looking up at the ceiling as he tried to fight back more tears. *This is so like Ofunneka*, he thought.

She apologised in the letter for all the pains she had caused him. She wrote that she spent time dwelling on his extramarital affairs and the pains this caused her. She never took time to appreciate him for the wisdom he demonstrated by making sure that the children turned out alright. She said what she learnt most from him was to be happy no matter the circumstance. She believed that he would do just that. In her absence he should just move on. She asked him to get himself a companion if he cannot cope alone and to feel free to remarry. Lastly, the letter gave

Amah detailed instructions on where and how to find everything that would be required for her funeral.

Ofunneka belonged to many charitable organizations and societies in and outside the Church. She had reached out to so many other people in different ways and had paid for the tuition and upkeep of many students in various schools. Although Amah knew that his wife was kind and generous, it was only at the funeral that he began to realize the extent to which she touched the lives of people around them. The crowds that trooped to their home to pay their last respects included mothers, fathers and those she had counselled over the years. One young man said to her husband,

"Auntie Ofunneka was the first Bible I ever read. She carried herself so well that I decided to emulate her in so many ways."

She had put together a family album and videotaped many incidents in her life. There were pictures of her at every stage of life, her family portraits at every celebration. Her instructions were that: Everyone who attended her funeral should be in blue jean trousers or skirts and white T-shirts or blouses. She did not want anyone to weep and wail for her. She also asked that she be buried in her wedding gown. Her children were not to feel like it was the end of the world. Everything that happened, she said, had the hand of God. Same advice went for her husband. As for her mother, Otua, she was sure God would fortify her. She said hopelessness was for people who had no faith. With these words she soothed the minds of her loved ones even in death.

The burial ceremony was unprecedented. There was no black and no mourning. People wore jeans in different forms - three quarters, skirts and trousers. Some wore white tee shirts with Ofunneka's picture on it. Others wore plain white tops. The funeral took place at her husband's compound in Lagos where they lived. It was a large crowd that gathered to pay their final respects. The family did not prepare for such a large number of people. She had specified that small chops be served. No rice. No heavy food. Only snacks. Amah informed them to reflect their lives rather than hers, as she had instructed in her letter. She had mentioned that the guests should reflect on their own lives, not hers since she was gone: *I have lived my life and now, I am memory. No one should feel sorry for me, or my husband or children. All those who are present have their lives to live.* She wanted them to be happy at all times, because life is short.

Most of what she wrote in her message to her husband she also recorded in a video. This was played at the funeral alongside other videos and pictures of her life. As people listened and watched, some laughed, others shed a little tear, and yet others sobbed uncontrollably. It was her autobiography, the story of her life on earth.

All through the ceremonies, Ofunneka's children conducted themselves well. They did not cry or roll on the floor. When it was time for the family to give the vote of thanks, Ofunneka's pregnant daughter took the microphone:

"I'm sorry we're taking you through this. That's what my mother would say." This triggered a round of laughter from everyone. She continued, "We have come today to celebrate the life and times of a great woman. My mother is an unusual breed. I'm using present tense for her because she lives on. She lives in us, her children." She turned to address her stepfather. "Daddy, please raise your head. We've never seen this part of you and we do not want to see it again. I want to say this before everyone present; by all means if you're lonely get married. No one will condemn you. It does not mean you loved mother less. It is what she would have wanted. The story of your life will be incomplete without our mother's name. So, you don't need to be unmarried to prove how much you loved her; we know. Deal with your grief the best way you can and move on with your life, guided only by the spirit of God. To everyone here present, we say thank you for coming and for saying the sweet things you said about our mother. Today has been an eye opener for us. We promise to continue in her legacy the best way we can. Mother is incomparable but we believe a part of her is in us, her children. As you all go back to your various destinations, we ask the good Lord to grant you all journey mercies."

The gathering chorused, "Amen!"

As they departed, they carried her with them and as the sun slowly descended from the skies ushering in night, they set to life once more.

THE END

Acknowledgement

First and foremost, I will like to give God the glory, for being my best friend through thick and thin and for His profound unconditional love for me.

To my father, Chief Lucky Ossai Gabriel Ishiekwene, who taught me contentment and how to live lightly; my mother, Mrs. Silver Omede Helen Ishiekwene, who has groomed me not to give in especially when life's curves seem very sharp, I am eternally grateful.

My deepest appreciation goes to Olorogun (Barr.) Clement Ekwevugbe Djebah, my husband who does not throw my mistakes at me no matter how huge and completely loves me the way I am. He is the reason why I exhale!

As for my children, Oghenetega, Ubiukpe, Oghenero, Oghenemarien; I thank you all for unveiling me, thereby helping me discover hidden aspects of my being. Had it not been for you all, I would not know as much I do. Also Mrs. Maureen Khediehon, Ruemu and Jude.

To my parents-in-law, Chief P. B. Djebah and Chief Mrs. Martha Sanaye Djebah, who accepted me as their own daughter, I say "May God's favor never cease in your lives."

To my siblings Andrew Ishiekwene, Emma Ishiekwene and family; the journey of growing up together is soothing! Thanks.

I would also like to thank my clergy friends, priests and spiritual directors – Rev. Fr. Nicholas Djebah, Rev. Fr. Louis Odudu, Rev. Fr. Daniel Agbor, Rev. Fr. Ambrose Abaka Oghenejode, Rev. Fr. Michael Ogunniyi, Rev. Fr. Michael Kerekunel, Rev. Fr. Matthew Udoka and Rev. Father. Augustine Okeke – for their formidable support.

For friendship I wish to keep forever, enjoying their encouragement and inspiration, my friends of inestimable value, who open up their hearts and tell me the truth even if it hurts – I am grateful. They are Mrs. Barbara Ifeanyi Aligwekwe, Dr. Lilian Anwulika Okoro, Mrs. Obiageri Ogboma, Mrs. Esther Sekegor, Margaret Ofotoku, Dr. Priscilla Okeleke, Mrs. Benedicta Osubelle, Esther Ekere, Lady Glory Ugwu, Dr. Uwem Okome, Lady Perp-Paul Onwuzurike, Lady Yemisi Ojeh, Lady Gloria Obaze, Anthonia Jibunor, Ezinne Kufre-Elkanem and Lady Efe Ehikhuemen.

Speaking of encouragement, I must mention the following people who are my backup power pack – Prof. Onokome Okome, Barr. Margaret Adewale and Dr. Dave Ehikhuemen. To the following I say "Thank you" for your expertise in polishing the manuscript: Priscilla Nnaka, Dr. T. M. Edah, Dr. Charles Ugwu and Sir Victor Anazonwu.

I also appreciate Adeoye Oloruntobi, Tobi Kolawole and Kachi Onyeulo, who are part of my UNVEIL TEAM, for their boundless energies and commitment.

And to everyone else at JTI Core, friends and team too numerous to mention, I say thanks a million for being you and for being there for me.

About the Author

Philomena Bivese-Djebah (PhD) is a certified marriage counsellor. She is the founder of Joyful Tears Initiative, an NGO which focuses on helping women beat breast cancer. Her work with countless women battling the disease has led her to recognize a strong correlation between the quality of family relationships and breast cancer survival rates. In *Ofunneka*, she explores fiction as a means of capturing and sharing some of her deepest professional insights. She holds degrees in Theatre Arts, International Law and Diplomacy as well as Guidance and Counselling from both the University of Port Harcourt and the University of Lagos. She is married with children.